IN THE SHADOW OF GIANTS

Liam Monclair

IN THE SHADOW OF GIANTS:
Espionage and Corporate Conflicts in China

Table of Contents

Warning

This book tells the story of my life. It is an authentic story, based on real events that I experienced. However, out of respect for the people and companies involved and in order to protect their privacy, some names and details have been changed.

The facts recounted express my personal point of view, without any intention to harm or to infringe on anyone else.

Foreword

I am dedicating this book to the many men and women who work in the shadows of large multinational corporations. These invisible people, whose role is crucial, contribute to the economic success of these large companies, while protecting the reputation and sometimes even the lives of their leaders.

Often, their effort involves huge personal sacrifice. They are the silent guardians who face the crises, keep the lid on scandals, and make sure that the machine carries on running, out of the spotlight. This book is recognition of their contribution but also a glimpse of the complex reality of these lives sacrificed on the altar of ambition and performance.

This account is for them.

I Introduction

The Shanghai Parcel

Night had fallen in Huzhou when my telephone vibrated on my night-stand. I had only slept for two hours, exhausted from days of preparation for the next day's board meeting. My role was clear: to guarantee the security of the Altéone Group management in the face of the growing threat from Wang Industries, led by the elusive Mr. Wang.

My phone screen showed the name of Gabriel Lemoine, Asia-Pacific director of the Altéone Group. His voice, which was normally calm, conveyed unusual urgency.

"They have received a suspect package at the Shanghai head office. There is a letter in Chinese with it. 'Traitors, enclosed are chemicals.' That's all we have for now."

Immediately, I sat up. Shanghai was a two-hour drive away. Allowing the situation to get worse or calling the police could create a scandal that Wang Industries would unscrupulously exploit. I decided to take care of it personally.

I grabbed my medical kit and called one of our drivers to prepare the Mercedes S500. It wasn't just a car; it was a strategic tool, equipped to navigate quickly through the Chinese urban chaos. During the drive, I prepared myself mentally, calmly listening to Jay Z on my iPod. But every second counted.

Two hours later, I was standing outside the Altéone Group's offices, on the 19th floor of a modern skyscraper. Inside, the atmosphere was tense. My security team had blocked off the room where the parcel was. A slight chemical smell hung in the air.

I took a photo of the package and the letter before touching anything. Then, with gloves on, I cautiously opened the envelope. A short translation from one of the local agents confirmed the threats. "Traitors, enclosed are chemicals."

The telephone vibrated again. Gabriel Lemoine, on the line again.

"You can't open that parcel. It's too risky."

"Calling the police would cause more damage. I'll take the risk. Stay on the line."

With surgical precision, I opened the package. My heart was pounding like crazy, but my training kicked in. Inside were receptacles containing chemicals. Nothing explosive, luckily. I took photos to document every step, and I secured the objects.

At four o'clock in the morning, once I had finished my task, I arrived at the Shanghai Ritz-Carlton to rest for an hour. I fell into bed and stared at the ceiling, unable to get any real rest. The pressure of events was weighing on me, but I knew that I needed to leave again soon.

So, one hour later, I left the hotel and drove back to Huzhou. Two more hours driving, still deep in thought, my hands gripping the steering wheel as the sun started to appear on the horizon.

Back in Huzhou, I arrived just in time to get to the Hyatt Regency, where the board meeting was to take place. I changed quickly and headed to the room where Gabriel Lemoine and the team were waiting. Tired, but determined, I knew that it was going to be a long day and that this was just the start of the conflict with Wang Industries.

The quiet luxury of the Hyatt Regency, which I knew well, stood in strong contrast to the pressure that was weighing on my shoulders. I swiftly made my way down the corridor, getting a few curious stares, but most of the hotel guests seemed to be engrossed in their breakfasts or in their business discussions. For them, it was a day like any other. For us, it was a battlefield.

In the private meeting room, Gabriel Lemoine was waiting for me, as was Patrice, the legal director for Asia-Pacific, and a few other people from the management team. The atmosphere was serious. The large table was covered with documents, maps, and laptop computers. The air was loaded with adrenaline.

"Well?" asked Lemoine, when he saw me come in.

I set the printed photos and the report on the table.

"No explosives. Just staged to intimidate us. But they used chemical products to heighten the threat. The letter, when translated, is direct: They want us to pack up and go." Patrice, his face tense, clenched his teeth.

"Wang is playing with fire. He wants to frighten us, but he knows that the police won't do anything. This is his territory here."

I nodded. Wang's power was omnipresent. In China, he was more than just a business owner: He was an almost mythical figure, with support in all circles of power.

At 8 a.m., as the board meeting was starting, a large crowd of protesters was breaking new ground. They had grown in number. There were now around fifty or so of them at the hotel entrance, shouting out slogans and waving banners. What had been a disorganized gathering the day before was starting to reach a worrying size.

My team, posted inside, followed the movements of the protesters on the security monitoring screens.

"Boss, they are trying to get in through the main entrance doors," one of my agents told me through my earpiece.

I immediately left the meeting room to go down to the ground floor. The situation was more serious than I thought. Some of the protesters had forced their way in and were now in the foyer, shouting their demands. The hotel guests, panicked, were trying to hide or to leave the hotel.

I had no time to lose. The security of the Altéone management team was the priority. I called Gabriel Lemoine, who was still in the conference room.

"We need to get everyone out of here, now."

Lemoine hesitated for a beat.

"But where do you want us to take them?"

"We're going back to Shanghai. That's the only place where can get some control over the situation. I already have a plan."

He trusted me, as he always did.

I immediately coordinated the evacuation. A discreet exit was impossible with so many demonstrators around. We needed to use a strategy to distract them.

I used a small team to simulate activity around the hotel's secondary entrance. The protesters, alerted by the excitement, gathered around that point, which allowed the main group to evacuate through the underground parking lot.

Down in the basement, three cars were waiting for us, their engines running. I had taken care to choose unmarked vehicles, which would be impossible to distinguish in the Huzhou traffic.

"Quick, get in," I ordered.

The directors, with their assistants, got into the cars. Gabriel Lemoine, Patrice, and two other managers climbed into the vehicle that I was driving myself.

The drive to Shanghai wasn't easy. As we were pulling away from the Hyatt Regency, I noticed two scooters in my rearview mirror that seemed to be following us.

"They're tailing us," I said to Lemoine, who was sitting beside me, and he went pale.

"What should we do?"

I quickly made a decision.

"We change routes. Warn the other two cars by radio."

I took a sharp left turn at a crossroads, taking a quieter road. The scooters tried to follow, but in the confusion, we lost them.

In order to ensure the convoy's safety, I told the lead car to slow down a little, while we checked at each junction. Once we were sure we weren't being followed, we got back onto the freeway that led to Shanghai.

When we reached the city, we weren't taking any risks. The convoy headed straight to a secure hotel, the Ritz-Carlton, where we had already organized a temporary lockdown area for the managers.

Once the cars were parked in the basement, I helped Gabriel Lemoine and the others to get out.

"We'll stay here for at least two days," I said calmly. "There's no way we're going back to Huzhou while the situation is out of control."

In the privacy of their hotel suites, the managers could relax at last. During that time, I went over the Huzhou video camera footage that the security team had sent us. The crowd had been dispersed by the local authorities at last, but the incident clearly showed the escalating tensions.

I immediately contacted our legal advisors in China.

"This incident is a red line. We need to send a clear message to Wang Industries. They can't be allowed to cross that line."

But deep down, I knew that the battle had only just begun. Wang Industries never backed down.

Under Pressure in Shanghai

The Shanghai air was particularly heavy that day. As I arrived in the underground parking lot of the Shanghai Ritz-Carlton, I felt tiredness weighing me down. I hadn't slept properly for almost forty-eight hours, but the situation hadn't given me respite.

Once the managers were safe in their suites, I took a few minutes to make sure all the security measures were in place. The hotel had been chosen for its infrastructure: high-definition cameras, limited access to the VIP floors, and discreet staff used to dealing with sensitive clients.

I hurriedly gathered my team together in a private meeting room.

"Listen carefully," I said, laying a map of Shanghai on the table. "Wang Industries know that we are here. I want every access point to be monitored, every delivery checked, and every movement documented."

They nodded. The team, made up of experienced former military and security personnel, knew the rules. But I had to remain vigilant. Wang Industries played on many fronts, and their capacity for infiltrating or manipulating a setting was formidable.

At around 3:00 p.m., as the managers were having a late breakfast in one of the hotel's private dining rooms, I received a call from one of my agents posted at the main entrance.

"Boss, we have an unplanned delivery. The driver is insisting on taking it up."

I frowned. Unplanned deliveries were cause for an immediate alert.

"Don't let anyone through. Block the access and keep them with you. I'm on my way."

Once I got there, I found a man in a courier's uniform, holding a medium-sized box. He looked nervous.

"Who sent you?" I asked him in Mandarin.

"It's a delivery for one of the guests," he replied, avoiding eye contact with me.

I knew that something wasn't right. I carefully took the box and brought it into a secure room to inspect it. With my latex gloves and my portable detector, I quickly detected an anomaly: The box contained a modified electronic device. Was it a bomb? A listening device? I wasn't taking any chances.

"Call the police," I ordered my team. "And put the guy into an interrogation room."

When the local authorities arrived, they confirmed my suspicions. The box contained a sophisticated listening device, designed to intercept communications across a wide range of frequencies. A maneuver that was typical of Wang Industries, who were trying to gather sensitive information on our strategies or our movements.

The courier was interrogated by the police and ended up admitting that he had been paid cash to deliver the box. He didn't know the sender's identity. A dead end, but it clearly revealed to us how intense their campaign against us was.

In spite of this incident, Altéone's strategic board meeting had to go ahead, the aim being to define the next legal and business response in the face of Wang Industries' provocations.

Seated around a glass table in a room that was out of sight, the directors had a heated debate. Gabriel Lemoine and Patrice, the key figures in this meeting, were clearly tense.

"We can't stay silent after what they did in Huzhou," said Stéphane. "Media pressure could play in our favor if we expose their methods."

"But that could also work against us," replied Lemoine. "China doesn't like foreign companies posing as public victims."

I hang back, listening closely while keeping an eye on my tablet screens. The direct feed from the hotel cameras showed that everything was calm, but my instinct told me that something was brewing.

Right in the middle of the meeting, Lemoine's telephone vibrated. It was an unknown number, but he decided to answer. The call was short, but strange enough to alter the atmosphere in the room.

"That was a representative of Wang Industries," he murmured, setting his phone down. "They want to organize an informal meeting."

The whole room felt silent. Everyone knew that these "meetings" were rarely innocent.

Wang Industries was probably trying to negotiate an agreement, while consolidating its position.

"We can't refuse," Stéphane said finally. "But we need to prepare in case it's a trap."

Then I spoke up for the first time since the start of the meeting.

"If this meeting happens, I want total control of the environment. Nobody moves without my say-so, and every detail must be scrutinized with a fine-tooth comb."

The meeting was set up for the next day, in an inconspicuous restaurant in the center of Shanghai. The team and I spent all night securing the scene. Hidden cameras, reconnaissance of the exits, and the strategic placing of agents were part of the protocol.

I visited the restaurant beforehand, talking to the manager to make sure that no outside employees would be present. Every table, every chair, every object was inspected. Wang Industries was unpredictable, but I wasn't going to give them any breathing space.

The next morning, as the managers were preparing for the meeting, I remained on guard. Wang Industries had shown its ability to create distractions, to infiltrate our spaces, and to strike where we least expected.

In this silent war, each decision, every movement counted. And I knew that the slightest error could cost us dearly.

Wang Industries: The Rise of an Emblematic Company

Wang Industries is a company that was founded in 1987 in Huzhou by Mr. Wang, a visionary entrepreneur. In its early days, Wang Industries was a small cooperative that sold products for schools, and children's products in particular. Under the leadership of Mr. Wang, the company had quickly grown and become one of the largest industrial groups in China, producing a wide range of mass consumer goods.

Wang Industries managed to take advantage of the explosive growth of the Chinese economy in the 1990s and early 2000s. It positioned itself as a vital national player, with effective distribution even in rural areas. The company became a symbol of Chinese economic success, incarnating both modernity and a certain traditional aspect in its marketing and business approaches.

In the 1990s, as Wang Industries was experiencing rapid growth, Mr. Wang had tried to find foreign partners to speed up the growth of his company. In 1996, the French group Altéone, one of the world leaders, had entered a partnership with Wang Industries. Together, they had created a co-company (a joint venture), where Altéone owned 51% of the shares and Wang Industries 49%.

This partnership seemed promising: Altéone brought its international expertise, its capital, and its technology, while Wang Industries contributed through its brand, its distribution network, and its in-depth knowledge of the Chinese market. In theory, this alliance would allow Wang Industries to become a world leader and Altéone Group to strengthen its presence in China.

But in spite of the appearance of a harmonious partnership, tensions had started to appear between Altéone and Wang Industries. The main source of conflict was to be found in a fundamental difference in their visions and their ideas of control.

The first sticking point was related to brands outside of the joint venture company. Indeed, Mr. Wang, alongside the joint venture, had carried on operating the Wang Industries brand through other companies that he controlled personally, without the involvement of Altéone. These companies, known as "non-joint companies," produced similar products to the joint venture and also used the Wang Industries brand. This allowed Wang to retain a certain independence, while taking advantage of the benefits of the joint venture.

Altéone, for their part, estimated that this constituted unfair competition and a breach of the terms of the initial agreement. The French group considered that the Wang Industries brand should be used exclusively in the context of the joint venture company.

The second problem was to do with control of the joint venture. Mr. Wang was feeling increasingly frustrated at the influence of Altéone, who owned a majority of shares (51%). He accused Altéone of wanting to control Wang Industries and restrict its growth, while not knowing about the specifics of the Chinese market. Wang also stated that Altéone was trying to take control of the "non-joint companies," which he saw as an attempt at a foreign takeover.

The conflict then had a cultural and nationalist dimension. Because Mr. Wang had cunningly played to nationalist Chinese feeling to rally public opinion to his cause, presenting Altéone Group as a foreign company that was trying to exploit an emblematic Chinese brand. This strategy resonated powerfully in a China that was becoming increasingly aware of its identity and economic sovereignty.

In 2007, the conflict between Altéone and Wang Industries ended up coming to a head. Altéone had taken Wang Industries to court, in China and internationally, accusing Mr. Wang of breaching the initial agreement and illegally using the Wang Industries brand through his "non-joint companies." Mr. Wang responded with similar accusations, stating that Altéone wanted to take full control of his company and that he himself was defending Chinese national interests.

The conflict had soon snowballed in the media, becoming an emblematic case of the difficulties of foreign companies working with local partners in China. It also brought to light the difficulties posed by cultural differences, diverging views of partnerships, and the often-incompatible ambitions of the two parties.

My role in the conflict between Altéone and Wang Industries was clear: to protect our teams in China, to safeguard sensitive information, and to coordinate the international inquiries related to the dispute. It wasn't just a matter of strategy, it was a silent war, where every move needed to be precisely calculated. Working closely with large international law firms and private intelligence agencies, I was at the crossroads of diplomacy, law, and operational intelligence.

When I had taken on the role, the climate was tense. Wang Industries had intensified its efforts to destabilize Altéone, employing various methods from aggressive media campaigns to more subtle maneuvers of surveillance and intimidation. The first priority was to guarantee the safety of our managers and the teams involved in resolving the conflict. In China, threats can be direct or more insidious.

Every journey was meticulously planned. I organized secure convoys, chose hotels with reliable infrastructures, and put in place strict protocols to avoid any information leaks. For example, during strategic meetings in Shanghai, every room was systematically inspected to detect any listening devices. My teams and I worked closely with local experts, trained in the realities on the ground.

One of the most critical moments was when we discovered a suspicious parcel sent to the regional head of office of the Altéone Group in Shanghai. While the team on the ground was dealing with the situation, I was in constant contact with our regional director, Gabriel Lemoine, and the relevant authorities to ensure a fast, discreet response. This kind of incident was not rare in the tense climate and showed the need to remain vigilant at all times.

Beyond China, my role stretched to managing international conflicts linked to the dispute. The legal battle between Altéone and Wang Industries was not restricted to just one territory. The ramifications reached the United States, Europe, and several tax havens, where crucial information needed to be gathered to reinforce our legal position.

I worked directly with some of the biggest international law firms, such as Lexon Partners or Bradley & Spire, who managed the legal aspects of the conflict. My role was to provide them with the information required to build a solid case against Mr. Wang, the head of Wang Industries and its parallel companies. This included gathering financial documents that proved embezzlement of funds, locating Wang's assets abroad, especially in the United States and the British Virgin Islands, and finally, identifying Wang Industries' strategic partners who were supporting its illegal operations.

Each investigation required meticulous coordination between the private intelligence agencies we had hired, the investigators on the ground, and analysts specializing in economic intelligence.

To achieve our objectives, I worked with some of the best private intelligence agencies, companies that were used to sensitive operations in hostile environments. These experts brought specific skills, such as infiltration of organizations, professional surveillance, or in-depth analysis of complex data.

For example, one particularly delicate mission consisted in following the movements of certain key members of the Wang family in the United States. I remember a conversation with the head of a Los Angeles–based agency, in charge of carrying out surveillance of their properties. We needed to obtain specific information about their assets, without ever crossing any legal red lines. That required meticulous planning but also in-depth knowledge of local laws to avoid any false moves.

Another operation took place in the British Virgin Islands, where we had to meet a source who claimed they had information on Wang Industries' offshore accounts. I coordinated this mission remotely, in constant communication with our agents on the ground, while making sure that lawyers supervised every step to ensure the investigation's integrity.

Although logistics and strategy were at the heart of my work, the constant pressure of the conflict could never be ignored. Every decision I made had major implications, not just for Altéone but also for the individuals involved on the ground. I needed to juggle between the need to get results and the responsibility of protecting our teams.

I remember a particularly striking moment during a meeting with our legal advisors in New York. A lawyer looked me right in the eye and said to me, "You realize that if this information were to be leaked, it could ruin the whole case?"

This kind of reminder of reality was everywhere. In this world, the slightest error could cost millions or even compromise years of work.

Working on this dispute allowed me to work with world-renowned experts, to learn to navigate between the mysteries of international law, and to further my skills in crisis management. It was an experience that was both exhilarating and exhausting and one that left an indelible mark on my career.

In this world of shadows and power games, I understood that the key to success lay in precision, anticipation, and trust in the teams. Altéone was not just a company: It was a giant whose every move needed to be protected in a merciless battle against Wang Industries.

The Enigmatic Mr. Wang: A Titan with a Human Side

Mr. Wang, the boss of Wang Industries, is a person of many paradoxes. At sixty-seven years old, he is not only the richest man in China but also an industrial hero. His story is a legend in the Chinese economic landscape, a source of inspiration for millions of young entrepreneurs who dream of building an empire. Yet, this billionaire magnate, at the head of one of the largest beverage companies in the country, remains a man of disarming simplicity. Simplicity that could easily deceive.

Unlike other figures in the business world from influential families or prestigious universities, Mr. Wang started his career at the bottom of the ladder. In the 1980s, when China was only just emerging from the economic reforms of Deng Xiaoping, Mr. Wang was selling ice cream at the gates of Huzhou factories. A simple little cart, staple goods, and ironclad tenacity: These were the first tools of his rise.

It was on this basis that he built the foundations of Wang Industries, a company that would come to dominate the Chinese market. Over the years, Mr. Wang grew his company from a simple local stall to a global empire, rivalling international giants like Coca-Cola and Pepsi. What sets Wang Industries apart from other companies is its ability to capture the essence of Chinese consumer needs, offering them products that are suitable, accessible, and reliable.

In spite of his colossal fortune, Mr. Wang never adopted the traditional codes of the Chinese economic elite. Where other magnates show off their wealth with luxury cars, sumptuous villas, or designer clothes, Mr. Wang is strikingly understated. He dresses like a Huzhou worker, gets around in a family Buick van – a utility vehicle that is more often associated with expats than billionaires – and seems to prefer direct human relationships over ostentation.

In his company, Wang Industries, he likes to be surrounded by women. Not because of vanity but because he believes that they bring the balance and the emotional intelligence required in management. His employees describe him as a demanding but fair boss, who can charm with his simplicity while impressing with his vision.

My first encounter with Mr. Wang was during negotiations at Huzhou, at the Hyatt Regency, with Gabriel Lemoine, a strategic partner. As I was waiting in a room adjacent to the meeting room, a man entered discreetly. He was wearing such simple clothes – an ordinary beige shirt and worn socks – that I mistook him for Mr. Wang's chauffeur. He had a modest, almost unassuming way about him, which didn't reflect his status at all.

Lemoine, who was already in the meeting room, asked me over the phone if Mr. Wang had arrived. I confidently replied, "No, not yet." It was only when Lemoine stuck his head out the door to check that we realized our mistake. The man I had ignored, thinking that he was just an employee, was indeed Mr. Wang. His simplicity had made him unrecognizable, and he seemed almost amused by my confusion.

My second encounter with Mr. Wang was just as telling when it came to his character. It took place in the Shanghai Hilton, in the hotel's huge foyer. That evening, I was in the jazz club that was just off the foyer, listening to a black American singer performing the classics with a friend. The atmosphere was cozy and intimate, until a noisy, visibly drunk group burst in.

Clumsily making their way down the central staircase, a large group of well-dressed men were laughing loudly and leaning against each other to stop themselves from falling over. At first sight, they seemed to be executives enjoying a company party. But one detail caught my attention: They were wearing ID badges with the Wang Industries logo. Curious, I followed them at a distance, and the middle of this joyous chaos, I recognized Mr. Wang.

Unlike his drunk colleagues, he remained quiet and methodical. While the others were struggling to walk to their chauffeur-driven cars, he made sure that each of them got in safely. He helped them with remarkable patience, calling the drivers and guiding them towards the cars. It was only once he was certain that everyone was looked after that he got into his own vehicle: a Buick family van, identical to the one I used myself as an expat.

For me it was a striking moment. Seeing a man in charge of an empire of several billion dollars more concerned about the well-being of his staff than his own image. That humility and that attention to detail go some way towards explaining why he was so respected, even beyond economic circles.

Mr. Wang is a living paradox. On the one hand, he is a man with formidable ambition, a strategy that has challenged the biggest names in world industry to establish the domination of Wang Industries. On the other hand, he incarnates a humility and a simplicity, which are almost unreal for a man of his standing. This duality makes him a fascinating character, both anchored in everyday realities and driven by an extraordinary vision.

If Wang Industries is a major force in China now, it's because Mr. Wang has always known how to embody his company: pragmatic, accessibly and deeply rooted in the needs of ordinary people. But behind this simplicity hides fierce intelligence, a man who knows more than anyone that true power lies in the details – even those that nobody else notices.

This simplicity and pragmatism, which seemed almost out of place in the often-flamboyant world of Chinese magnates, were no doubt the key to his success. For me, meeting Mr. Wang was a lesson: proof that, sometimes, the most powerful figures are also those stay most in the background.

Shadow Play

When you hear about Altéone, you imagine an industrial company that is the leader in its field. What few people realize is that, behind this smooth image, Altéone Group is also a huge multinational, with strategic interests in markets where competition is brutal. In China, it's not just a matter of market share: It's a war. A war of influence, where every decision is a battle, every error an opportunity for the enemy.

I must admit that when I accepted the position at Altéone, I felt a certain personal pride, and also family pride. My grandfather Robert had carried out his compulsory military service alongside a man who was to become a legend in the business world: Pierre Lacheray, the historic, visionary founder of Altéone.

According to my grandfather's stories, they were not just friends but also barrack buddies. Lacheray, who was already charismatic and daring, dreamt of a future that would transcend borders. My grandfather remembers his passionate speeches about industry, about the idea of creating products that would be consumed by millions of people. These conversations, in modest military dormitories, stuck with my grandfather, as they still stick with me now.

I often wondered what Lacheray would have thought of this corporate war in China. The man who believed in cultures coming together would no doubt have been torn by this conflict. But I also knew that he would have approved the need to defend Altéone's vision against adversaries as tough as Wang Industries.

Altéone had underestimated Mr. Wang at the start. Thinking that a strategic partnership with Wang Industries would open up the doors to the Chinese market, the company had massively invested in a joint venture. But what started as a mutually beneficial collaboration turned into an open conflict. Wang accused Altéone of wanting to control Wang Industries. Altéone for their part criticized Wang's attempts to create parallel companies to funnel away profit.

And my role in all this? To protect Altéone's interests, in every respect: physical, legal, strategic. That meant organizing the managers' security, managing risks in relation to travel to sensitive areas, but also carrying out much more subtle missions.

In China, competition is not just a question of numbers or commercial strategy. It's a struggle, where anything goes. Industrial espionage, orchestrated media campaigns and alliances with local authorities are all part of the game. For Wang Industries, Altéone Group was the foreign enemy, the interloper who was trying to assert themselves on territory that didn't belong to them.

I remember my first mission related to Wang Industries. It was in Shanghai, during a strategy meeting between our local teams and international consultants. A few days before the event, we had received a warning: an anonymous email notifying the presence of "foreign traitors" and promising to "ensure China's honor was respected."

It wasn't an isolated threat. The tension was palpable. Wang Industries, without ever directly committing themselves, used go-betweens to create a climate of fear. Groups of protesters rose up in front of our offices. Defamatory rumors appeared in the Chinese media. And sometimes it took on darker forms: Staff were pressured, confidential information seemed to leak as if by magic.

Working for Altéone in this context meant navigating a permanent gray area. My team and I weren't just protectors: We were players in a complex game, where every move needed to be calculated.

Mr. Wang was a formidable adversary. His presence weighed on each decision we made. I had not met him at that stage, but everything that I knew about him fascinated me. He had a unique ability to manipulate perceptions. In the eyes of the public, he was a patriot, a man who was defending Chinese industry from foreign "invasions." For us, he was a merciless strategist, ready to use any means to achieve his objectives.

My daily routine was anything but routine. One day I might be coordinating security for an Altéone director during a trip to Beijing. The next day I could be organizing tailing someone in Los Angeles to monitor a partner suspected of sharing sensitive information with Wang Industries. Another time, I was taking part in a strategy meeting in Paris, in a hushed room where every word was weighed like a weapon.

Every moment, I had to be ready to anticipate the unpredictable. But it wasn't just a matter of security. It meant understanding cultural dynamics, political subtleties, and economic factors. In China, everything was connected. A simple interpretation error could cost millions or compromise years of investment.

I knew that every mission had its share of danger. Wang Industries was playing to win, and they had the resources to hit hard. But I also know that we had our strengths. With a devoted team and a keen sense of strategy, we could not only survive but also make progress.

II My Beginnings and Training

Forging Steel

My life had never followed a predefined path. Every step was the result of an opportunity seized, a challenge overcome, or a stroke of luck that had been decisive. What led me to work for a multinational company like Altéone goes back to long before I knew what I wanted to do with my life.

I come from a family where hard work is not an option but rather a necessity. My father was an emigrant from Senegal, a man of extraordinary intelligence and determination. In spite of his modest beginnings, he had obtained two doctorates, one in physics and the other in economics. But to reach that level, he had had to overcome obstacles that most people can't imagine.

For years, he had worked as a night watchman to meet our needs, while studying at university during the day. This infernal pace never seemed to tire him out. He often said, "In life, we have no excuses. If you want something, you do what it takes, period."

He instilled that rigor in me, that sense of duty. But he was also extremely hard to please. I was disciplined for any error on my part, anytime I didn't meet his expectations. And his blows, although indefensible, left a positive mark on my flesh and my spirit. They taught me to never give up, even under pressure or pain. Even now, I can feel that discipline in my actions, in my way of never backing down when faced with a challenge.

After my military service, I wanted to see what I was capable of. Not just physically, but mentally too. I had always been drawn to travel, discovering new cultures, and challenges that would allow me to go beyond my limits. That's what brought me to Dengfeng, a town situated not far from the Shaolin temple, but best known for its sports schools.

These schools take only the best pupils, who come from all over China, and sometimes abroad, to learn martial arts, reinforce their discipline, or who are just looking for something bigger than themselves. I was one of them.

Every morning, at sunrise, we went running in the mountains that surrounded the town. The fresh air, the shouts of the trainers, and the noise of our shoes against the ground created a unique atmosphere.

I still remember the endless lines of boys and girls, some of them very young, running with fierce determination.

The exercises were brutally simple: run, climb, jump, repeat. But what struck me most was the collective energy. It didn't matter if you were tired or if your legs were giving up on you: The encouragement from the other pupils and the trainers pushed you to carry on.

It was in Dengfeng that I received my first lesson on China and its unique perception of the time. Every day, after training, I went to buy a bottle of water in a small local store. The first day, the shopkeeper asked me for 100 yuans for a small bottle. I paid without protest, thinking that this was the going rate in that region.

The following month, the price went down to 70 yuans, then 50 yuans, then 20 yuans. Each time I went there, the price went down, without me saying a thing. It was only after six months that I started paying the real price: 2 yuans, the price that all the Chinese had been paying all along.

That experience, once I got over the initial surprise, led me to understand a fundamental truth: Time in China is not really experienced in the same way as in the West. Where we look for quick, immediate results, the Chinese favor a patient, sometimes almost imperceptible, approach. They test, observe, and adjust, but at their own pace.

In that situation, the seller wasn't just trying to maximize his profits: He was building a relationship. Through the slow price adjustment, he made sure I understood how they did things and above all that I kept coming back. From that I took that, in their culture, time is a tool. The Chinese don't hurry; they master time like a craftsman forging raw material.

This lesson would prove valuable in my career. In China, everything, from business negotiations to strategic alliances, rests on a way of managing time that can unsettle impatient foreigners. And above all that, in order to succeed, you need not only to respect their pace but you also need to learn to understand it and adapt to it.

Once back in the West, I knew that I needed a solid education to transform my experience into practical opportunities. I joined the business management program at HEC business school in Montreal. It was a totally different environment, a mixture of theory lectures, practical projects, and fierce competition between students.

But what really made me stand out was my ability to manage stressful situations. During simulations of negotiations or team projects, I was often the person who stayed calm and found a solution.

That was when I took my first steps in corporate security. A former class-mate from the Naval School, who worked for a private military company, asked me to join his team. The contrast, in that environment, was striking. One day, I was working on a strategic marketing project; the next, I was monitoring a sensitive industrial site in a conflict zone.

At Dengfeng, I had learnt physical and mental rigor. At Montreal HEC, I had acquired the necessary tools to navigate in a world where decisions were made in conference rooms but where instinct and determination were still essential. These experiences, even though they seemed to be complete opposites, in fact complemented each other perfectly and were later to define my role in a universe whose existence I wasn't even aware of yet: the world of corporate espionage.

The School of Discipline: The Parachutists

Having grown up in a demanding family and having lived my experiences in Dengfeng, I found myself taking a step that would sculpt my mind: becoming part of a parachute regiment in the south of France. This choice wasn't just a way of serving but also a personal quest to test my physical and mental limits in a setting where failure was not an option.

The training was relentless. Every day felt like a test just to survive: long marches day or night, heavy packs, never-ending exercises in the blazing sun or in freezing cold weather. But nothing really prepared me for the visceral fear that I would feel before my first parachute jump.

The regiment had its traditions, and one of them was the songs. Every exercise, every parade was punctuated by the military melodies, intoned by the leader or the parachutists themselves. The most memorable song for me was the one that our commander sang before every jump: "Through the Door".

It was a song of black humor, which set out, with biting irony, all the ways you could die jumping out of a plane:

Through the door,

The wind was blowing so hard,

A cord that breaks, a canopy that tears,

Adieu, friends, I'm dead.

The words described scenarios where the equipment would fail, the wind be treacherous, or the parachutist would make a fatal error. It could have felt demoralizing, but on the contrary, that song brought everyone together. It was a way of recognizing the risks, laughing about them, and showing that in spite of everything, we were ready to face them.

The commander, with his deep, powerful voice, sang the first lines, and soon the whole plane was ringing with soldiers' voices. It was both terrifying and rousing, a kind of ritual that prepared us for the inevitable: jumping into the void.

On the day of the first jump, everything felt unreal. The plane, noisy and filled with palpable nerves, vibrated in time to the beat of my heart. When the song "Through the Door" rang out in the metal cabin, I concentrated on the commander's instructions: position, timing, equipment checks.

When the light went green, everything sped up. The line inched forward slowly, all the men disappearing one by one through the open door of the plane. Then it was my turn. My hands were clammy, my breath ragged. My mind was screaming at me not to jump, but my body, almost automatically, followed the instructions.

I jumped into the void, and for a fraction of a second, the whole world stopped. There was no more noise, no more fear, just a suspended moment in the vastness of the sky. Then the brutal shock of the parachute opening brought me back to reality. The ground was coming at me fast, and I needed to prepare for impact.

That first jump transformed me. It taught me that fear is inevitable, but that it should never paralyze us. All it takes is one step, one gesture to overcome it, and once that's done, you realize that it doesn't have power over you any longer.

Of the many events at that time, there is one that I will never forget. During a training jump, my chief officer, a man who was both feared and respected, took me to one side just before we boarded the plane. He was holding two glass bottles of beer.

"Monclair," he said, in a serious voice, "these beers are going in your pack. I want you to bring them back intact after your jump."

I was astounded. It wasn't a request: It was an order. While the other soldiers were loading their gear, I was packing two beers, getting amused looks from my friends.

During the jump, all I could think of was the moment when I would touch the ground. I imagined the bottles breaking, and the adrenaline within me mixed with an absurd fear of disappointing the officer. When the impact came, I did my best to cushion the shock and protect my precious "equipment."

Once I reached the ground, I immediately checked: The bottles were intact. Proud of my exploit, I gave them to the officer. He inspected them, raised them as if for a toast, and said with one of his rare yet sincere smiles, "Well done, Monclair. You deserve your rest today."

Although this exercise may seem absurd, it taught me something important: Whatever the circumstances, regardless of the pressure, you need to know how to protect what matters. In this specific case, it was beers. But later in my career, it would be lives, secrets, or strategic interests.

Other than the jumps, the training in the regiment was a real schooling in resilience. The long marches, often at night, were particularly challenging. Loaded with a pack that sometimes weighed almost 40 kilos, we had to march without asking any questions. Every step felt like a mountain to climb, but there was no room for giving up.

I remember one freezing cold night when we walked for hours without a break. My legs felt heavy, my shoulders crushed under the weight of the pack, and my mind was toying with the idea of giving up. But something inside me, the discipline my father had inculcated in me, the mindset that Dengfeng had sharpened, pushed me to go on.

When we finally reached our objective in the early hours of the morning, the officer shouted in a sarcastic tone, "You're all still alive. That proves it wasn't so hard."

In that moment, I understood that the body is always stronger than the mind believes. Limits are things we impose on ourselves. And things we think are insurmountable become possible when we refuse to give up.

These experiences in the parachute regiment forged me. They taught me to face my fears, to deal with pressure, and to find solutions in situations that seem desperate. Above all, they gave me unshakable confidence: the confidence of knowing that whatever the challenges to come, I had the strength and the tools to overcome them.

Diving into the Shadows

The world of corporate espionage was not a path I had planned. It was a universe I discovered almost by accident but which very quickly had become a vocation. It all started with a meeting in a Parisian café, but it was in Carcassonne, between the train station and the 3rd Marine Infantry Parachute Regiment, that my real training began, at the head office of Secopex, a private military company headed up by the legendary Ewald Wolfle.

My first encounter with Ewald was in Paris, in a café opposite the Gare de Lyon, called Aux Cadrans. Ewald Wolfle, former sergeant major in the 3rd Marine Infantry Parachute Regiment, had twenty tours and a twenty-year career behind him. His reputation was legendary in military circles: a man of iron discipline, known for his leadership and his composure in the most dangerous situations.

When I walked through the door of the café that day, I saw him immediately: imposing, focused on a file that was open in front of him, with a black coffee beside it. He looked up as I approached him.

"Monclair?" he asked, in a neutral tone of voice.

I nodded. He closed the file and gave me a piercing stare, then came straight out with "Do you know what you want to do in life?"

I explained what motivated me: my thirst for learning, my desire to find a field where action and strategy went hand in hand, and above all my desire to play my part in things that matter. He listened attentively, nodding his head from time to time, before setting down his coffee and replying with a direct tone of voice, "Very good. I will set you up in Carcassonne, above the Secopex offices. It will be modest, but you will be at the heart of everything. If you want to learn, it starts there."

A few days later, I arrived in Carcassonne, a town marked by its military history and by the presence of the famous 3rd Marine Infantry Parachute Regiment, where Ewald had served for two decades. The Secopex head office was midway between the train station and the regiment, a strategic location that seemed almost symbolic.

Ewald set me up in a little studio just above the offices. It was modest, as he had said, but functional: a bed with a firm mattress, a small table, and a window overlooking a quiet street. To me, it was perfect. It allowed me to be completely immersed in that world, to learn directly from Ewald and elite operators who regularly came to the offices.

The studio became my base, a space where I could think, work on administrative missions, and take in all that was said in the rooms below. The discussions, reports of operations, and preparations for missions were all valuable lessons.

Ewald, faithful to his reputation, was demanding and precise.

"Monclair, this job is not for people who are hesitant. Here, everything you do, even behind a desk, has an impact on the ground. If you don't understand that, you haven't understood anything," he declared on my first day.

He immediately involved me in administrative and logistic preparation of missions. My work consisted of organizing files, drawing up contracts, and coordinating the operators' needs. But Ewald also made sure that I understood the reason behind each decision.

During a meeting with a client, who wanted to secure an oil facility in North Africa, he let the man talk for a long time about his expectations. Then he intervened, very calmly, saying, "You're not hiring us to solve a problem. You hire us so that there are never any problems. That's our job."

These words struck a chord with me. They sum up the essence of this job: prevent, anticipate, and act before crises arise.

Living over the offices meant that I never really left work. The elite operators who came through Secopex often shared their experiences with me in the evenings. These tales were fascinating: extracting hostages, negotiations in war zones, or even securing convoys in hostile environments.

Once, an operator told me, "A good mission, Monclair, is one where nothing happens. Not because there are no threats but because we have neutralized them before they are even visible."

These words taught me the importance of anticipation, a principle that was going to be central to my way of working.

The days passed, but they were all different. Ewald always found ways of setting me challenges, whether that was through sending me to meetings, asking me to manage complex logistical aspects, or trusting me with strategic analysis.

Every task, every conversation, and every observation helped me to understand that this job was not just an extension of the army. It was a whole other universe, where strategy, diplomacy, and implementation had to exist harmoniously.

The little studio over the Secopex offices was much more than modest accommodation. It was the starting point of a transformation. It was there that I learnt the basics, absorbed tales of those who had experienced the most extreme situations, and forged the skills that would serve me throughout my career.

When I left Secopex to follow my own path, Ewald shook my hand with his characteristic smile at the corner of his mouth, and said, "You have what it takes to do good work, Monclair. Remember, in this job, you always need to be one step ahead."

Those words, spoken in Carcassonne, would resonate in every decision I would make from then on.

Iraq: Sabotage in the Desert

Iraq, with its sand stretching to infinity and its strategic infrastructures dotted within hostile areas, represented a unique challenge. Here, threats could come from anywhere: from the sky, the ground, or shadows in the night. It was in this very tense context that I found myself on a mission near Bassora, on an oil complex that had suffered a series of sabotages. But I wasn't taking on this mission all by myself. By my side was a man whose presence imposed respect. Mike, a sixty-year-old man from South Africa, seemed to have lived through all the wars and survived all the conflicts. His experience was legendary, and his piercing stare spoke of stories that were never to be told.

Mike was a former South African military man, probably a veteran of the Angolan war, although he never confirmed that directly. Like a lot of men of his generation, he had served in conflict zones all over the world, forging a reputation as a clever tactician and an implacable operator. Rumors did the rounds about his past as a mercenary, from African jungles to the mountains of the Balkans, but he remained mute on that subject.

Tall, sturdy, with a square jaw and a deep voice, Mike was the kind of man who imposed a sense of calm by his presence alone. He always wore a worn khaki cap, which seemed as old as him, and carried a military knife attached to his belt, even when he was in the field.

He didn't speak much, but when he did, his words were direct, precise, and full of practical wisdom.

"You know, Monclair," he said to me one evening around a campfire. "In this job, the difference between living and dying is often just a detail. And details are what most people forget."

On the fourth night on-site, we were doing a round together. The silence of the desert was only interrupted by the whirr of the generators and the sound of our footsteps in the sand. The air was heavy and oppressive, filled with tension that we could almost feel physically.

As we passed an isolated section, a flashing light caught my attention. One of the surveillance sensors had been deactivated. Mike, in a heartbeat, realized the urgency.

"Let's split up," he said simply. "I'll take left, you take the right. Stay alert."

I knew that Mike never gave orders without thinking them through. His voice was calm but firm, and that was enough to reassure me, even though my heart was racing.

As I moved through a dimly lit area, a blueish glow caught my attention. As I carefully got closer to it, I saw the outline of someone crouching down, fiddling with a mobile phone. My blood immediately ran cold. The telephone wasn't just a communication device.

It was an improvised detonator, probably connected to an explosive charge placed close to the pipeline.

I stopped about ten meters away, slowly drawing my Glock 17, which I aimed directly at him. My breathing got faster, but I forced myself to remain focused.

The man looked up and saw me. His eyes, filled with anger and fear, met mine.

"Set that telephone down!" I ordered in a firm voice.

But he didn't understand. His face clearly showed me that he didn't speak English. My words felt pointless, replaced by the silent tension of that duel. He squeezed his telephone more tightly; it looked as though he was hesitating between fleeing and pressing the button.

At that moment, I was more frightened than him. My finger was resting on the trigger, ready to fire if necessary. But I knew that just one wrong move could unleash a catastrophe. Fear screamed at me to fire immediately, but my instinct told me to wait, to read his gestures, to find another way out.

Every second was filled with tension. The slightest movement, the smallest change in expressions, became vital information. Sweat was pouring down my face, and my hand shook slightly, even though I forced myself to remain steady.

All of a sudden, a shadow appeared behind the man. It was Mike, who approached soundlessly, like a predator tracking its prey. In a rapid, precise move, he grabbed the man by the neck and disarmed him, tearing the telephone from his hands before pinning him violently to the ground.

"Keep your arm aimed at him," groaned Mike, glancing in my direction.

I kept my Glock 17 aimed at the man, my finger still ready to act. Mike, who was unshakable, quickly inspected the phone.

"Active detonator," he said, deactivating it with impressive speed. "This guy knew what he was doing, but not enough not to get caught."

Once the zone was secured and the explosive device defused, Mike straightened up and looked at me.

"You did well, Monclair," he said, a smile only just perceptible at the corner of his mouth. "But remember, in these situations, patience saves more lives than bullets do."

Those words, simple but full of meaning, resonated with me. That night, I had learnt a valuable lesson. Fear, even though it can be intense, is not a weakness if it is controlled. It is a constant reminder of the importance of each decision.

The next day, at the debriefing, Mike was true to himself: calm, level, almost detached. Under his apparent indifference was a man who had seen everything and faced everything. He was not looking for glory or for recognition. For him, every mission was just another day in a life where the combat never ended.

Leaving Bassora a few weeks later, I knew that this mission had changed me. Not only through the intensity of events but also through the presence of Mike, the man who embodied experience and composure. His words and actions stayed with me, as did the night we had avoided the desert becoming a tomb for both of us.

Jakarta: The Art of Observation

When I arrived in Jakarta, I was immediately struck by the raw energy that this bustling megalopolis gave off. The streets were teeming with life, horns answered each other with a constant din, and scooters darted about in all directions, forming a chaotic ballet. Everything seemed to be on the brink of implosion, but inexplicably this precarious balance worked. The air was heavy, filled with the smell of asphalt heated by the sun, smoke from street food grills, and a tension that was hard to define. Jakarta was not just a city. It was a living, pulsing, unpredictable organism.

Unlike my missions in Iraq, where the danger was tangible and immediate, this challenge was being played out in a much more insidious arena. Here, there were no explosions to dodge or shots fired. But the risks were every bit as real, hidden under a layer of seeming normality. I could already feel that this city was going to leave an impression on me, not just through its physical dangers but through the complexity of the intrigues that it housed. What I didn't know at the time was that it would never really let me go.

My mission was for a security company based in Singapore, which was specialized in high-risk environments. A multinational company, operating in the manufacturing sector, was victim to growing trade union issues. The protests were getting larger, and the underlying tensions led us to believe that we could expect targeted violence, in particular against expat managers of the company. My role was clear: to infiltrate that unstable environment, to identify the union leaders, to understand their motivations, and above all, to anticipate their next moves.

The subtlety of this mission was in the context. One blundering gesture, one word too many, and the situation could explode. Every interaction had to be measured, each movement calculated. The playing field was a powder keg, and my mission was to map the fuses.

During a particularly tense trade union meeting, a crowd had gathered in front of company headquarters, brandishing placards and chanting slogans in a crescendo of anger. I observed the scene from a distance, blending in with a group of local observers. Any little detail could be revealing: Leaders rarely fear those who shout loudest but rather those who direct the chaos with almost unnoticeable precision.

That's when I saw it. Unlike most of the demonstrators, the man was hanging back, calm and focused. He was methodically handing out pamphlets, exchanging furtive glances with other people in the crowd. He wasn't wearing clothes that stood out or any signs of political affiliation. He blended into the background, but his gestures showed unusual control. He wasn't there to express personal frustration. He seemed to be orchestrating the scene.

Intrigued, I decided to follow him discreetly. Slipping through the crowd, I forced myself to keep a reasonable distance so as not to raise suspicion. At one stage, he stopped in an alley to exchange a few words with another man, holding a document case. I observed more closely, and there was a detail that jumped out at me: he was wearing an earpiece, hidden under his hair. My instinct was confirmed. He wasn't an ordinary demonstrator. He was someone trained, perhaps a go-between for a larger organization.

I carried on shadowing him, my thoughts spinning as the pieces of the puzzle came together. Who was this man? Did he work for a local political faction or a competitor company, or did he have ties with outside forces that were trying to destabilize the region? These questions added a layer of uncertainty to an already dangerous mission.

Jakarta had a unique way of playing on your nerves. The smothering heat weighed on my shoulders, and the humidity made my shirt stick to my skin, accentuating my discomfort. The constant horns, the intent stares of passersby, everything seemed to be conspiring to stop me keeping my cool. But in this commotion, I had to stay focused. Failure was not an option, not on a mission where the consequences of an error could be measured in lives lost.

That evening, I went back to my hotel, exhausted but unable to lower my guard. Every phone call I received, every movement in the corridor felt suspicious. Jakarta is not a city where you can become complacent. It wrapped you up in its web of uncertainty, and even moments of respite seemed to be tinged with danger.

As I took off for my next destination, I watched the lights of Jakarta disappear on the horizon. The city seemed to have left an indelible mark on me, a constant reminder that some places never really let you leave. And over the following months, it would try to keep this promise in a way I could never have imagined.

My mission was over, and I felt a mixture of relief and foreboding. I had completely achieved my objectives, but part of me knew that it wasn't over. This city, with its streets teeming with people and its relentless energy, seemed to be calling to me to come back, as if it hadn't finished testing me yet. The complex dynamics that I had only just started to untangle had left a door open to a future that I couldn't ignore.

The man with the earpiece, his methodical gestures and his obscure role in the demonstration, had left me with more questions than answers. Alongside my main task – identifying the trade union leaders and understanding their motivations – a new mystery had been added, which threatened to overshadow my results.

It was only when I went back through the reports that I had fed back to the security team that things started to become clearer.

A few days after I left, I received a cryptic phone call from my contact in Singapore. "We dug a bit deeper into the information you gathered," he told me, and his voice had an edge of contained urgency. "Your man with the earpiece... he's not just a local go-between." Cross-analysis of data showed that the man I had followed had unexpected connections. He wasn't a trade union leader, nor just an ordinary observer committed to the workers' cause. In fact, he worked for an economic intelligence company based in Hong Kong. Their role? To provide multinationals in competition with strategic information – or put more simply, to sell to the highest bidder details that could destabilize their rivals.

By infiltrating the demonstration, he was collecting evidence that could be used to make the company's position more fragile in the Indonesian market, probably in the interest of a direct competitor. The pamphlets he was giving out were not as innocent as they looked: subtle messages, carefully chosen sentences intended to exacerbate tensions and to encourage an escalation of the conflict.

My instinct had been right, but that was just the surface. What I didn't know at the time was this person was not acting alone. By digging a little deeper, my contact found a sprawling network: economic intelligence consultants, local lobbyists, and even corrupt members of the Indonesian government seemed to be involved. The goal was clear: to force the company in question to make huge concessions or to push it to reduce its business in Indonesia, which would leave room for its competitors.

What I had thought of as a mission purely about trade union tensions was turning out to be part of a much larger game. The trade unions were just a pawn in that game. The real players were pulling strings in the shadows, manipulating genuine frustrations of the workers to serve private interests.

I couldn't help but wonder: What more could I have done? Should I have insisted on digging deeper into this man, so that we could have understood the links earlier? These questions, as is often the case in my job, remained unanswered. The objective of the mission – to defuse the immediate situation and protect the expatriates – had been achieved. But this victory seemed hollow in the face of the complexity of what we had found out.

In the end, the company decided to strengthen its security measures, while starting careful negotiations with the trade unions. The influential network behind the demonstrations was placed under surveillance, but the power of those forces remained too widespread for a direct action to be undertaken. In this kind of conflict, there are no clear triumphs. Just adjustments to survive the next storm.

Observing Jakarta from the plane that day, I understood that this city had a lot more to offer than its obvious chaos. It was a mirror of global issues: struggles for influence, crossed interests, and ordinary lives caught between forces much larger than them. This mission had taught me never to trust what is visible on the surface. Behind every façade there is a hidden world of intrigues, and one simple detail – an almost imperceptible earpiece – can reveal a much larger and more dangerous picture.

Israel: An Extraordinary Training Ground

This visit to Israel, my second, marked an important stage in my career. Unlike the first time, when I discovered this fascinating country, this time I was here to improve my skills. This wasn't my first training session in close protection but a specialization, which was supposed to perfect my techniques in high-risk environments and expose me to even more realistic scenarios.

Israel, with its world-recognized expertise in matters of security, was the perfect place to improve. Each aspect of this training course had been designed to push participants to their limits, and I knew that these two weeks were going to be some of the most demanding of my career.

Landing at the international Ben Gurion airport, I was immediately plunged into the unique atmosphere of the country. The Israeli security services, renowned for their vigilance, welcomed me with their well-known methods. When they saw my first name, which is Arab in origin, they decided to test me.

An agent shouted to me, "You know, Mr. Allaoui came here for a visit last month."

Mr. Allaoui was a Syrian businessman that I had protected in the past. This statement, which was unlikely given where my client was from, was clearly meant to test my reaction. Thanks to my previous training, I understood their strategy perfectly. They were trying to analyze my expressions, my responses, to detect any possible lies. Remaining calm, natural, and indifferent was the key. I easily passed their test.

This first contact reflected the culture of rigor and the high standards that would mark my entire stay here.

I arrived in Israel three days before the start of the training to acclimatize and to enjoy Tel Aviv. This city, with its dynamism and its open-mindedness, was the antithesis of the stressful environments that I was about to face. Between the golden beaches and lively markets, I found some peace of mind.

The nights in Tel Aviv, which were vibrant and joyous, were a welcome interlude before the intensity of the training. The inhabitants, who were always welcoming, shared their enthusiasm for this city where modernity met well-established traditions. Those few days were perfect to recharge my batteries.

The training took place in a kibbutz situated midway between Tel Aviv and Jerusalem. The setting, which was very different to the luxury hotels I was used to, represented getting back to basics. A kibbutz, a colony based on sharing and solidarity, is an experience in and of itself. The members live without individual possessions and share everything, from farming resources to daily tasks.

Living in this community for two weeks brings a refreshing simplicity to things. It was a way of focusing fully on learning, far from the usual distractions.

The training was divided into two parts. It went beyond the basics I had learnt in previous training courses, going into more detail with each skill and adding complex scenarios to test our limits.

- **First week: advanced basics**

  - **Advance detail:** Prepare the arrival of a client in an unknown place by identifying potential threats.

  - **Convoys and formations:** Coordinate vehicle movements in an urban environment.

  - **Reconnaissance and detection of explosives:** Training on how to anticipate attacks.

  - **Shooting and Krav Maga:** Perfect self-defense and neutralization techniques.

- **Second week: realistic simulations**

The training took place in urban settings in Tel Aviv and Jerusalem, where we had to protect a "client" in complex and sometimes unpredictable situations. Each exercise combined stress, the unexpected, and coordination between the members of the team.

During a particularly intense exercise, an incident occurred. A bad fall in a close protection scenario left me with an acute pain in the shoulder and a suspected serious injury. The trainers, who were always professional, immediately stopped the exercise and decided to take me to one of the hospitals in Tel Avis for tests.

That trip to the hospital was an eye-opening experience. In spite of the tension and fatigue, I was struck by the way the members of the medical team worked together. Israeli Jews and Arabs worked together with efficiency and smoothness that seemed to rise above the divisions that we often hear about in when we are outside the country. This cooperation, which felt almost natural in the context, surprised me and gave me an insight into Israel that was different from what we see in the media.

Fortunately, my injury didn't require any major intervention. The next day, I was able to get back to the exercises, but more carefully this time.

Jerusalem, with its spiritual and historic depth, was at the heart of one of the most memorable experiences of this training course. My grandfather had often told me about this city, describing how important it was and advising me to go there one day. When I first got to know it, I finally understood what he had meant.

During an exercise in the old city, we were escorting a client after a visit to the Wailing Wall. As we were going back up the Via Dolorosa, a road that is filled with symbolism for Christians, the emotion was palpable. This path, marked by Christ's Passion, resonated with a historical and spiritual significance that transcended differences in faith.

As I was walking up the Via Dolorosa, my phone vibrated in my pocket. It was my mother. But because of the strict protocol of the training course and in order to respect the intensity of the moment, I didn't answer. It was only when we got back to the kibbutz, late in the evening, that I took the time to call her back.

Her voice was calm, but filled with emotion.

"Your grandfather passed away today."

That news turned an already serious training course upside down. The city itself, with its deep spirituality and unique atmosphere, seemed to be with me in mourning.

The team, made up of Jews and Catholics, shared mutual respect with regard to the spiritual abundance of Jerusalem. Each place of worship we visited seemed to be filled with a kind of magic that it is hard to describe: a melting pot of cultures, architecture, and histories that left a lasting impression.

This time, Israel didn't just give me new skills. Obviously, our time there was delving into a world where every detail counts, where instinct and training come together to guarantee security. I left with a clearer vision of what is involved in close protection in high-risk environments.

But this experience also left a mark on me personally. It strengthened my respect for this complex country and gave me rare chances to reflect, in particular in Jerusalem, where the weight of history and spirituality seemed to entwine with my own family history.

When I left Israel, I knew that this training course would not only improve my career but that it would also leave an indelible mark on my personal life.

Gunsite: Under the Unforgiving Arizona Sun

It was the middle of summer when I arrived at Phoenix International Airport; the burning air hit me as soon as I stepped out of the terminal building. The thermometer read well over 40°C, and even in the shade, the heat was suffocating. The Arizona desert is merciless, and every breath of air seemed to me hotter than the previous one. But this hostile climate was the perfect prelude to what was in store for me: total immersion in the demanding universe of Gunsite, the legendary shooting range.

After picking up a hired car, I took the road to Prescott, around two hours to the north. The drive was spectacular: from the urban bustle of Phoenix to the raw solitude of the desert. The landscape changed quickly, from flat, arid stretches to rocky hills punctuated by giant cacti. The road, edged by canyons, plunged me into the isolation of the area.

During the drive, I saw signs warning of rattlesnakes. These creatures, camouflaged among the rocks, represented a constant danger for anyone who went off the beaten track. At Gunsite, I was soon to learn that in addition to the rigors of training, the desert itself required constant vigilance.

Arriving in Gunsite for the first time is like entering a sanctuary dedicated to firearms. The center, which spreads over acres of arid desert, combines modern infrastructure and raw nature. The shooting ranges stretch as far as the eye can see, surrounded by hills that amplify the echo of shots.

The instructors, all former military or special forces experts, had undeniable presence. Every word they said, every instruction they gave, carried the weight of their experience. Here, there was no room for improvisation or complacency.

The days began at dawn, as the sun started to warm the desert. And from ten o'clock in the morning the heat became overpowering. The sand and the rocks under our feet were burning, making every movement more difficult. Drinking water became an absolute necessity to avoid dehydration. Even the equipment we carried seemed to weigh twice as much in this furnace.

Firing in bright sunlight added another dimension to the challenge. After a few hours, the heat made the temperature of the weapons rise to almost unbearable levels. The cases, ejected after each shot, annoyingly often slipped into our shirts or our sleeves, burning our skin before we could get them out.

The thousands of shots we fired every day created a ceaseless noise, a constant hammering that seemed to fill the very air itself. The hearing protection was little defense against the deafening racket. But it was the noise of the RPG rocket launchers that really sticks with you: a powerful blast and a booming explosion that shakes everything around it, reverberating in the surrounding hills like a clap of thunder. Firing with a weapon of that scale wasn't just impressive, it was a visceral experience.

The training was not confined to fixed targets. At Gunsite, everything was designed to simulate real situations. The instructors thrust us into complex scenarios, where any error had immediate consequences.

One memorable exercise consisted of crossing a narrow canyon, shooting at targets that rose up unpredictably. Every echo, every shadow played games with your mind, demanding absolute concentration. The slightest moment of distraction could mean that you missed a critical target or, worse, hit a "civilian" represented by an innocent silhouette among the targets.

During another exercise, we had to defend a perimeter from a simulated "attack." The munitions, albeit blanks, produced a noise and a sensation that were close to reality. Tense muscles, fast breathing, you could feel the adrenaline rising. This kind of simulation teaches you to master your emotions, to remain calm even under intense pressure.

Ever since I was a child, shooting had always been a large part of me. My grandfather, with patience and precision, had taught me to handle a .22 long rifle in the fields near where we lived. These memories, full of simplicity and pleasure, had been my first steps into this world. But at Gunsite, this passion became a keen skill.

The emphasis on mental discipline and respect for weapons resonated deeply with me. Every weapon is a tool but also a responsibility. The instructors insisted on the importance of never letting your ego guide your decisions. "A weapon doesn't forgive arrogance," they would often say.

After each exhausting day, I went back to the family who were putting me up on their farm near Prescott. The contrast between the intensity of Gunsite and the serenity of these evenings was striking. The father of the family, always armed with his Colt 1911, liked to share his stories and his life lessons over a good meal.

His collection of weapons, meticulously locked away in a room at the back of the house, was impressive. He told me about each piece with passion, explaining its history, its mechanism, and its role in past times or modern conflicts. These discussions were like a prolongation of my training, offering different insights into the world of arms.

Gunsite was not just a training center. It was a forge where we sharpened our skills but also our characters. Each shot fired, every decision taken in urgency, the heat of the desert, and the weight of silence between two shots, all of that is impossible to forget.

Leaving Gunsite after this session, I knew that what I had learned here wouldn't remain in the desert. These skills, these reflections, and this philosophy would be with me on every mission, every challenge, and even in my day-to-day life. Because Gunsite is more than a place; it's a rite of passage.

A Dive into Complexity

When I arrived in Shanghai, I had already navigated in complex environments in several regions. Freelance work had sharpened my instincts, pushed my limits, and forced me to adapt to situations where the stakes and the expectations were high. But I could feel that my journey was about to take an unexpected turn.

The mission that had brought me to Shanghai seemed banal at first sight: supervising the improvement of security protocols for a regional head office. But this city, with its mix of ancient secrets and fast-moving modernity, had its own unique way of transforming the ordinary into something much grander.

The last day of the mission had been long. Late in the evening, the regional director, Gabriel Lemoine, offered to take me to Pudong airport. In spite of his formal, composed appearance, Lemoine gave me the impression that he was someone whose mind was always ten steps ahead.

During the journey, something unexpected happened. He took the time to talk – not about the mission or logistics aspect, but about me.

"You managed this operation remarkably well," he said pensively. "But what I'm more interested in is your way of thinking. You see things that other people miss. That's rare."

These words resonated with me as we reached the airport. Before I got out of the car, he added, "When you arrive, go and see the HR department at head office. I want to see you in Shanghai next week. Permanently."

It wasn't a request. It was an order – one that I hadn't imagined.

My flight back from Shanghai was AF111, a flight that I ended up getting to know by heart. It took off from Pudong at 22:05 and arrived early in the morning in Paris-Charles de Gaulle. I have taken this flight so many times that I could describe it in detail with my eyes closed. I knew exactly when the lights of Shanghai would disappear behind us, when the dimmed lights of the cabin would encourage passengers to sleep, and especially when – flying over Russia – the mobile network could be picked up.

That precise moment, often in the early hours of the morning, was a routine for me: checking my messages, sending emails, and preparing mentally for what was waiting for me. This intimate knowledge of the details of the flight is testament to the crazy pace that was going to become my new normal.

When I arrived in Paris early that morning, I was tired but alert. I had only just collected my luggage when my phone vibrated.

It was Gabriel Lemoine. His voice was calm, but his tone was firm.

"Take a taxi. Go straight to head office in La Défense. The HR director is waiting for you."

There was no hesitation in his words. And there wasn't any in mine either. I got straight into a taxi at the airport.

When I arrived at the prestigious building, everything felt unreal to me. I was greeted by an assistant who immediately escorted me to a conference room where the director of human resources was waiting for me with a contract that was ready to sign. No long speeches, no unnecessary formalities.

Once the contract was signed, the HR director, who was watching me determinedly, stopped for a moment to tell me something that would come back to me later, even if I didn't pay attention to it at the time,

"You know that it's not normal to be so close to power and to do so much when you are so young. When all this action and excitement stops – because it will stop – take care of yourself. Because you could get depressed."

I smiled, thinking that he was exaggerating, and went on to something else. But later, those words would come back to haunt me, because he was right.

Holding my contract, I took another taxi and headed home. I needed to pack my bags urgently for an immediate departure. Between throwing a few clothes into my suitcase, I took a moment to go and hug my mother.

"Are you leaving again already?" she asked me, worried but used to my fast-paced life.

"Yes, to Shanghai," I answered simply.

The next day, at dawn, I was back in a plane again, heading towards China. The contrast was striking. Less than twenty-four hours after landing in Paris, I was off again, this time to settle there, in a role that would change the course of my career.

I arrived in Shanghai early in the evening. The organization had made sure to reserve temporary accommodation for me at the Hilton, located near the Xingye Center, at the heart of Pudong. The hotel, which was modern and discreet, would be my base as I got used to my new role.

The view from my room, overlooking the twinkling lights of the skyscrapers of Lujiazui, seemed almost unreal. But there was no time to admire the scenery. The next day, a series of meetings was planned to fully integrate me into the team and to instill in me the responsibilities that were in store for me.

This time, I was no longer there as an external consultant. I was part of it now, with more responsibility. What was ahead of me was not just a mission but a deep dive into a world where security was just one of the many aspects on a complex chessboard.

This hurried return and meteoric entry into a large company as imposing as the one I was joining told me that the pace wasn't about to slow down. Shanghai was just the start. This experience would allow me to navigate around a much vaster and more complex world than anything I had experienced so far.

I didn't yet know where this new stage would lead me, but I was ready to dive in, heart and soul.

III The Escalation of the Altéone-Wang Industries Conflict

The Virgin Islands and the Pact with Archibald

When the plane began its descent to the British Virgin Islands, the view from my window took my breath away. Below me, an infinite stretch of white beaches with turquoise water, so clear that we could see the coral covering the seabed. It was a scene of paradise, in total contrast to the tension of my mission. However, I knew that, under this stunning beauty, there were dark hidden secrets.

It all began in New York, a few months before, during a previous mission, which had thrust me into the impenetrable world of offshore companies. Archibald, a contact I had developed at the time, had turned out to be a precious ally. A man of the shadows, he moved with almost frightening ease in the mazes of tax havens, shell companies, and camouflaged money transfers. His ability to unearth critical information on complex financial structures has made him a legend among those in the know.

Archibald was not an easy man to read. He was British and introduced himself as an independent consultant, but his work went far beyond that bland title. He had that rare gift of being able to break down complex financial systems into simple diagrams, finding the flaws and anomalies with surgical precision. But what really made him stand out was his network of contacts, forged through years of furtive transactions in places where confidentiality was a tacit rule.

During our last meeting in New York, he had hinted that he had crucial information on the financial cogs of Wang Industries. In particular, he claimed to have access to the company's offshore bank accounts, as well as clues to the real owners of the structures hidden behind them. He also knew that this information was worth a small fortune and that it could play a decisive role in the dispute between Altéone and Wang Industries.

But Archibald was not the kind of person who shared what he knew without substantial compensation. He wanted an exchange in person, in an isolated place, far from prying eyes and potential listeners. That was how I found myself in the British Virgin Islands, with a mission of gathering this sensitive data in exchange for a cash sum.

The destination was not a coincidence. The British Virgin Islands are a notorious tax haven, a place where billions of dollars circulate through a dense network of shell companies and anonymous bank accounts. A perfect setting for Archibald, who excelled in exploiting these gray areas of the worldwide financial system.

At Road Town airport, everything seemed to slow down. The passengers calmly disembarked the plane, some of them barefoot, others in relaxed clothing, as if they had left any notion of urgency behind. This almost hypnotic pace reminded me why Caribbean islands are often chosen as havens by those who are trying to hide – or hide something.

Our hotel, nestled in an isolated creek, was a gem of private luxury. The main building, with sun-bleached white walls, stretched the length of a beach with sand so immaculate it almost felt unreal. The rooms, small independent villas, faced the sea. Each villa had its own terrace, where hammocks swayed gently in the breeze.

The interior of my villa was elegant yet simple: stone walls, immaculate sheets, and a ceiling of sculpted wood. A bottle of local rum was waiting for us, along with a handwritten welcome note. Through the bay window, I could see the waves breaking on the beach. There was a palpable serenity about the place, an impression of calm that was in stark contrast to my reasons for being there.

Steve was already on the terrace of the neighboring villa, holding a beer, watching the turquoise sea.

"If all conflicts could bring us here, I wouldn't be complaining," he said, laughing.

Steve was an enigmatic character, a figure who was both fascinating and disconcerting. Physically, he looked as if he had stepped straight out of a spy novel: an Englishman who was around fifty years old, with piercing eyes and measured gestures, always impeccably dressed in a slightly rumpled shirt and good moccasins. Steve had been living in Los Angeles for over a decade and cultivated an aura of mystery. In his office, meticulously framed photos told of a life that he deliberately kept in the shadows. You could see him posing beside well-known figures like Yasser Arafat, which pointed to a past in the hushed circles of British intelligence.

In spite of his relaxed demeanor, Steve had a way of speaking that gave away a mastery of nuances, an ability to evaluate a situation in an instant. With his typically British humor, he defused tension while maintaining a posture of constant vigilance. He only shared a little of his past, but his stories – often told with a touch of irony and a glass in hand – suggested a career marked by delicate missions and gray areas. He had the rare talent of disappearing in plain sight, attracting just enough attention to make people look where he wanted them to.

During our trip to the British Virgin Islands, Steve was both a guide and a wall of silence to me. He knew how things worked, the places, the kinds of people we would be dealing with. His presence created a kind of serenity; with him, even the riskiest situations felt as though they were under control. However, in his silences, you could feel the weight of stories never told – stories that shape men like him, used to navigating between truth and shadows.

The next day, while waiting for our meeting with Archibald, I decided to take advantage of the setting to do some diving. The hotel concierge recommended a local guide to me, but it was a different meeting that would mark that day. While I was preparing on the pontoon, a tall, tanned young woman approached; her smile was as bright as the Caribbean sun.

"Are you here to dive too?" she asked, with a singsong Australian accent. Her name was Emma. A traveler and seasoned diver, she had been exploring the Caribbean for several months. Intrigued by my discretion, she suggested that we discover a little-known diving spot, far from the tourist circuits. I hesitated for a moment, but something about her enthusiasm convinced me.

We set off on a small motorboat. Emma, who knew the place well, guided the captain towards a small uninhabited island, surrounded by steep cliffs. Once we got our equipment on, we dove into the crystal clear waters. Under the surface, the world was transformed. Multicolored fish swam among the coral, and majestic rays slid slowly over the sand.

Emma signaled to me to follow her, pointing to a dark opening in the rock.

What I discovered next felt like it came straight out of a story. A series of underwater caves, their walls covered with shimmering rocky formations, going down to the depths. Emma had explained to me that these caves had been used as hiding places by pirates in past centuries. Their booty, it is said, had been hidden in the caves. I don't know if these stories were true, but the mysterious atmosphere fascinated me.

As we were coming back up to the surface, Emma looked at me with a smile.

"You see, treasures aren't always made from gold. Sometimes, they're just this... moments."

I smiled back, but my mind was elsewhere. My treasure was on a USB key that I was due to get hold of that evening, and it was much less poetic than this magical dive.

When I got back to the hotel, the reality of my mission became my priority again. I thanked Emma for the unexpected interlude, but my concentration was fully turned towards Archibald. The meeting place, an isolated beach-front restaurant, had been inspected in minute detail. Every table, every chair had been checked. Steve, true to himself, had prepared an evacuation plan in the event of a problem. Because with this kind of mission, the unexpected was often the only certain thing.

The magic time in the caves already seemed very distant as I took on my new role: that of a coordinator of a mission where every detail counted. As I entered the restaurant that evening, I knew that the destiny of Altéone-Wang Industries could shift with just a few words, a few documents.

But for now, thinking of the turquoise water and the secret caves again, I allowed myself a smile. Sometimes, even in the middle of the most intense missions, life gives us unexpected glimmers of light.

The sun had gone down on Road Town, and the lights of the beachfront restaurant gave a golden glow to the calm water of the bay. The setting was so peaceful that it seemed almost ironic that I was there for such a risky transaction. Steve and I had arrived twenty minutes early, as usual.

Archibald arrived at the exact time we had agreed. His walk was slow but assured, his face marked by years of a life in the shadows. He wore a rum-pled linen shirt and worn moccasins. His eyes were alert, scrutinizing every movement in the restaurant before he sat down facing me.

"You are more discreet than I thought," he said, as he sat down.

I just gave him a slight smile, preferring not to answer. In this kind of negotiation, not talking much is often more effective. Steve, sitting at a nearby table, kept an eye on us as he sipped his whiskey, ready to intervene at the slightest alert.

Archibald placed a small USB key on the table. It was ordinary, almost insignificant, but I knew that it contained information that could shake Wang Industries to the core.

"What you're looking for is here," he began, his voice low but firm. "Transactions, shell companies, and even clues as to their partners in Hong Kong. But I don't work for free."

"Nobody works for free," I replied calmly. "How much?"

He smiled at the corner of his mouth. He knew that he had the advantage.

"Two hundred thousand dollars. And I want a secure transfer."

I made a subtle sign to Steve, who nodded. The amount was high but not extravagant, given what this key could do for us.

"You'll get what you're asking for," I replied. "But not until I confirm that your information is worth that price."

Archibald leaned back in his chair, clearly satisfied. Steve stood up casually to take the USB key to our car, where a secure computer was waiting. In the meantime, I stayed facing Archibald, trying to detect any flaws in his behavior.

The silence stretched on, only interrupted by the sound of the waves and quiet laughter of the few restaurant patrons. Then my phone vibrated. A message from Steve came up:

"The files are legitimate. We have money transfers that match our suspicions. This is big."

I looked up at Archibald. He didn't seem nervous, but I knew that he was aware of the risks he was taking.

"So," I said finally. "You have kept your word. The transfer will be done within twenty-four hours. Remain available."

Archibald nodded, but before leaving, he leaned towards me a little.

"Just a piece of advice. Wang has powerful allies. If you think that this USB key is your ultimate weapon, you're mistaken. It's just a fragment. Prepare for repercussions."

And with those words, he left the restaurant, leaving me alone with my thoughts. He was right. Every step we took in this corporate war seemed to attract even more dangerous reprisals.

Back at the hotel, Steve and I delved into the files. What they revealed was damning. Massive money transfers, shell companies spread out all over the Caribbean and Asia, and direct links to companies in China that didn't appear in any official register of the Altéone-Wang Industries joint venture. This evidence was more than enough to strengthen our legal case.

But they also revealed a troubling reality: Wang Industries wasn't acting alone. Behind Wang, a complex network of local and international allies seemed to be orchestrating part of these maneuvers.

That changed everything.

"It's bigger than we thought," murmured Steve, his eyes glued to his screen. "If we move too quickly with this, they'll know that we're behind it and they will respond."

I nodded, staring at the columns of numbers and names on the screen. The real fight had only just begun.

The next morning, as I was sipping tea on the terrace of my villa, a hotel employee brought me an envelope. No signature, no sender. Inside there was a simple message written in block capitals:

"YOU ARE ON A SLIPPERY SLOPE."

I calmly folded the piece of paper and slipped it into my pocket. These threats weren't new, but their precision worried me. Someone, here on this very island, knew exactly what we were doing.

"We need to leave," I said to Steve, when I went to his room. "The longer we stay, the more we run the risk of raising the alert. We have what we need..."

Leaving the Virgin Islands a few hours later, I looked at the endless beaches one last time as they disappeared under the horizon. This magical place, where I had found underwater caves and shared those moments of unexpected calm, would now just be a memory mixed in with the tension of this mission.

Once we got back to New York, the evidence was immediately sent to our legal team. In a conference where tense murmurs resonated, the lawyers analyzed each document with surgical precision. One of them, after many minutes, turned to me.

"With this, Wang will struggle to defend himself. But be prepared; he won't go down without a fight."

I agreed. The war between Altéone and Wang Industries had just reached a new level, and I knew that the worst was yet to come. But we had just won a victory, and it was worth its weight in gold.

Mirror Effect

When I got back to New York, I found the hustle and bustle of Manhattan in stark contrast to the serenity of the Virgin Islands beaches. But there was no time for nostalgia. Archibald had kept his word, and the information he had provided was explosive. The ramifications were so wide-reaching that they required immediate coordination with law firms, investigators, and the strategic decision-makers of the Altéone Group.

In a hushed conference room in a Midtown skyscraper, the legal team analyzed the documents. The names, dates, and amounts on the screens showed a stark truth: Mr. Wang was not just an industrial visionary, he was also a master of dissimulation. Millions of dollars circulated through a complex network of shell companies, connecting Wang Industries to the financial centers of Hong Kong, Zurich, and the Caribbean.

But the triumph was tainted with apprehension. We knew that by revealing this information, we would trigger a reaction. Wang Industries, or the people who were pulling strings behind Wang, would not remain passive.

A few days after submitting the documents to Altéone's lawyers, we understood that the response from Wang Industries was there, but not where we had expected. In the morning, as I was drinking my tea in a coffee shop near Times Square, an urgent message appeared on my phone. An article had just appeared in a large Chinese media source. Its title, which was provocative, claimed "Altéone, a western parasite: How a multinational is exploiting China."

The sharp pen of the journalist left little room for doubt: Wang Industries had orchestrated this attack in the media. The text described Altéone as a colonialist company, accused of stealing local wealth. In this war of opinion, a coup like this could be enough to bring about a shift in public perceptions and to galvanize massive local support in favor of Wang Industries.

I immediately contacted Gabriel Lemoine, the regional director based in China. His usually composed voice was filled with stress.

"They are playing with fire. But we can't ignore this. There needs to be a rapid response, without falling into their trap."

A plan was swiftly elaborated. We would mobilize our communication teams, not to attack directly but rather to restore the facts via testimonials from local partners, with the aim of insisting on the positive impact of

Altéone in China. But in the background, it was clear that this war went beyond mere words. We needed to anticipate their next move.

The situation took an even more worrying turn a few weeks later. I had had to go to Shanghai urgently to supervise a strategy meeting with the Chinese lawyers and to coordinate the security of the Altéone directors. That night, exhausted by a day of intense discussions, I went back to my room in a five-star city center hotel.

The suite was luxurious, but every detail had been checked before I arrived: no hidden cameras, no visible threats. However, when I woke up in the early hours of the morning, one detail struck me immediately. My computer, which I had set on the desk, was open. I had closed it before I went to bed. I was sure of that.

My heart sped up. I quickly checked the content of the hard drive. A file with the code name "China" that I had created to confuse the issue had been opened. This file, however, didn't contain anything sensitive. It was just bait, a fictitious file meant to measure any attempts at intrusion.

I immediately contacted my security teams on-site. A rapid analysis of the suite revealed that someone had forced the electronic lock of the room during the night. Clean, precise work, but enough to confirm what I feared: We were being watched closely.

"The Chinese secret services, probably," murmured Gabriel Lemoine, when I told him about the incident. "They're playing this their way. Nothing happens here without their tacit agreement."

The next day, in spite of the tension, a crucial meeting took place in an unassuming building in the Pudong area. We had asked our Chinese legal partners to attend in order to examine the best strategy to adopt in the face of the new attacks by Wang Industries. The room, protected by strict security measures, held a dozen or so people, all concentrated on the implications of the documents obtained through Archibald.

"This evidence is enough to open an international inquiry," said one of the lawyers. "But if we use it now, it could inflame the situation even more."

"We must act," replied Lemoine, his tone icy. "We are already in an open war. If we do nothing, they will take that for weakness."

I remained silent, observing the tense faces around the table. Every decision we made here could have huge repercussions. And while the debate went on, my phone vibrated.

An anonymous message: "If you carry on, you won't leave Shanghai."

The threat was explicit. This time, it wasn't just a veiled threat. I signaled Lemoine to join me in another room. There, in a quiet voice, I explained the situation to him.

"We need to leave immediately. They know that we are here."

In less than an hour, we had mobilized a discreet escort to leave the office. Two unmarked cars were waiting for us in the underground parking lot. As we drove through the congested streets of Shanghai, I couldn't help but scrutinize every movement around us. Every scooter, every vehicle that seemed to be following us became suspicious.

We reached the airport without incident, but my adrenaline didn't settle down. I knew that this hurried escape was not a victory but rather a maneuver to gain more time. Wang Industries, or their allies, had clearly signaled to us that they were prepared to do whatever it took.

On my flight back to Paris, I took a moment to think. This war of influence, which had started with a typical legal conflict, had turned into an out-and-out battle. Mr. Wang, with his network of alliances and his mastery of local dynamics, was playing a dangerous game. But we still had cards up our sleeves, and every move had to be calculated.

As I stared out my window at the clouds, I realized that this was not only a fight for the company. It was a fight to prove that, in this shadow game, even giants can be shaken.

Shanghai

The Shanghai Ritz-Carlton, situated on the renowned Nanjing Shi Lu, was not just a place where I stayed during my missions in China. Over the years, this hotel had become a kind of second home to me. Its hallways were familiar to me, the staff greeted me with an almost complicit smile, and every detail seemed to have been thought of to make my stay as smooth as a well-oiled machine. This special link with the hotel was all the more precious as Shanghai, that teeming metropolis, imposed its crazy pace on every visit, making a reliable sanctuary more than necessary.

Shanghai is a city of contrasts. Puxi, where the Ritz-Carlton is located, embodies the history, the charm of the old narrow streets, the lively lilongs, where modernity and traditions come together. This is the beating cultural and historic heart of the city. The Nanjong Shi Lu, a vibrant main thoroughfare, remains a distillation of the soul of Shanghai: bright shop windows, a dense crowd, and the smell of street food in the air. A few kilometers from there, the Bund offers a spectacular view of the other side of Shanghai: Pudong, with its futuristic skyscrapers that seem to reach to the clouds.

From the terrace of the Ritz-Carlton, I liked to take in this duality. At night, the Bund became a vivid tableau: the art deco buildings of Puxi were lit up, and the skyscrapers of Pudong, like the Jin Mao and the Shanghai Tower, glittered like diamonds. This is a sight that sums up the very essence of Shanghai: a melting pot of the old and the modern, past and future.

On the lobby floor of the hotel, a Paul bakery added a European touch to my mornings. Every day, a piping-hot tea and a crispy croissant marked the start of a new battle. In a city where everything moved so quickly, this moment of calm was priceless. The smell of warm bread, mixed with the gentle background music, reminded me of Paris and gave me the strength to face the complexity of my missions.

But the Ritz-Carlton was more than just Paul. Its Chinese restaurant, with elegant décor and impeccable service, was my haven of peace after stressful days. There, I took comfort in my habits. As soon as I sat down, an attentive waiter placed a dish of Goubo Chicken in front of me and a bottle of Badoit sparkling water. This unchanging ritual, which was almost sacred, meant that the Ritz was much more than a hotel to me: It was an anchor in the storm for me.

But Shanghai is also a city that never sleeps, a maze of opportunities and dangers. Between two strategy meetings, I liked to escape for a few minutes behind the hotel. There, a small basketball court offered a welcome break. François, a young intern at Altéone, and I played improvised matches. His impeccable three-point shots and his constant humor made these moments a real escape from reality for me.

However, even in these lighter moments, Shanghai was always reminding me of its duality. It was a city where every smile can be hiding a strategy, where even the most ordinary encounters must be meticulously assessed. The constant pressure added to the intensity of my missions, but it was also one of the things that made life in Shanghai so exciting.

After exhausting days of tense negotiations, I went back to my suite on the 43rd floor. From the picture window, the city stretched out as far as the eye could see, its lights forming a hypnotic kaleidoscope. But on that evening, the beauty had an oppressive side to it. Although Shanghai was lively, it could also be intimidating.

On that evening, the streets, which usually teemed with electric scooters and hurrying pedestrians, felt more menacing. Each noise became suspicious, every face a possible threat. But we reached the airport without a hitch. As the private jet took to the skies, I watched the lights of Shanghai get further away. This city, with its complexity and inexhaustible energy, had left an indelible impression on me.

That's Shanghai: a theater where the comfort of the Ritz-Carlton meets the intensity of its streets, where every moment can switch from wonder to caution. With the croissants from Paul, the basketball games, and the incomparable view, it had become much more than a business trip. Shanghai was an experience, an adventure, a constant lesson.

Return to Paris: The Invisible Trap

Landing in Paris, after the tense events in Shanghai, was a temporary relief. The familiarity of the capital and the comfort of my normal environment reminded me that, in spite of the tensions, there were solid foundations that we could rely on. But the war with Wang Industries offered no respite. The next day, a strategy meeting was organized in our offices in La Défense, the economic heart of Paris.

The imposing building was an emblematic address, which reflected Altéone's prestige. In the conference room on the top floor, bathed in the light filtering in through the large windows, the atmosphere was studious. In turn, the French legal, strategic, and intelligence teams had started to examine the documents we had obtained through Archibald.

The international lawyers, after meticulous analysis, confirmed that the evidence collected was solid, revealing a complex network of shell companies, suspicious money transfers, and direct connections with offshore banks.

The evidence was actually enough to file lawsuits in several international jurisdictions. But a fundamental question remained: When and how to use this evidence? Launching a legal offensive immediately could trigger an unpredictable response on the part of Wang Industries.

"If we wait too long," Gabriel Lemoine said, by Visio conference from Singapore, "Wang will have time to cover his tracks. We need to strike now."

After hours of debate, a double strategy was adopted: filing the evidence in key jurisdictions, like Hong Kong and New York, while launching a behind-the-scenes campaign aimed at influencing public opinion in China, ground where Wang seemed to be ahead of us.

Alongside the legal process, I contacted a private intelligence agency based in London to monitor the movements of Mr. Wang and to anticipate his next steps. A few days later, I went discreetly to a town house in Mayfair, a chic, private area, with the aim of meeting their analysts.

In a sober but effective meeting room, a whiteboard was covered with maps and diagrams. The analysts exposed their findings with precision.

"Wang has intensified his trips between Hong Kong, Zurich, and Los Angeles," explained one of the agents. "He seems to be moving assets around in jurisdictions where the laws offer him more protection."

This information was crucial for our strategy. It revealed that Wang Industries was preparing for the storm that we were about to unleash. But it also suggested a certain vulnerability: Wang knew that he was under pressure.

On my return to Paris, I had a worrying surprise in store for me. Mail, left at the reception of the building in La Défense, with just my name on it. Inside, a photo: a blurred shot of me, taken in London as I got off the plane. Not a word, no explanation, just that picture. I immediately gave the photo to the security team. Their analysis revealed that the photo had been taken with a long-range camera, probably from a car parked near the airport.

"They know where you are," a security agent told me. "And they want you to know that."

This threat, albeit subtle, was a brutal reminder that every move was being observed. Wang Industries, or their allies, would not content themselves with having it out in court. They wanted me to know that their networks of influence were everywhere.

After a tense day, I decided to take some time for myself. In a small restaurant in the Marais area, where I sometimes met with close friends, I ordered a simple steak and French fries, with a bottle of Badoit sparkling water. This meal, along with the warm atmosphere of the place, allowed me to relax. That was when I received an unexpected phone call from François, the young intern from the Shanghai legal team.

"Sir, I just wanted to let you know that the team is still moving things forward here. You have our support."

His enthusiastic voice made me smile. François was young, but his commitment and his optimism reminded me what we were fighting for. It wasn't just a matter of profits or contracts. It was a matter of principles and values.

The next day, a decisive meeting took place in the Altéone offices. The goal was clear: to refine our strategy in order to hit Wang where it would hurt most, while mobilizing local support in China. We needed to show them that Altéone wasn't a foreign player but rather a partner committed to the growth of the Chinese market.

"Public perception is crucial," I explained. "If we can mobilize our local partners, we have a chance of countering Wang's influence."

This plan involved going back to Asia. But this time, it wouldn't be for secret meetings. It would be for a game of influence, where every word and every action would be strategic. Leaving the office that evening, I knew that the coming days would be decisive.

The battle against Wang Industries wouldn't be won all at once. But with each move, each maneuver, we were getting closer to victory. And in this shadow war, endurance remained our most powerful weapon.

Tennis Tournament

The tennis match was coming to an end, and the atmosphere in the ATP Shanghai Masters tournament arena was electric. The two players on court were giving it their all, and the crowd reacted to every shot with fervor. Sitting in the stands, I tried to get swept up in the magic of the game, but part of me remained on the alert the whole time.

Beside me, Katrin, the Swedish woman I had met a few weeks earlier at Bar Rouge, was fully enjoying the moment. With her roaring laugh and her sometimes stinging comments about the players, she brought a lightness that I had not felt for a long time. That evening, she had convinced me to take the pressure off and to let myself get into the spectacle.

"That player's going to win. I'll bet you a glass of champagne," she said with her melodious accent, pointing to one of the finalists.

I smiled and nodded, feigning a carefree attitude that I didn't really feel. The pressure of the last few days, the veiled threats from Wang Industries, and the incident with the protestors in front of the Ritz-Carlton were still weighing me down.

My phone vibrated in my pocket, and I apologized to Katrin and moved away a little to answer. On the line, François, the intern, spoke quickly, his voice sounding nervous.

"You need to get back to the Ritz-Carlton right away."

"What happened?" I asked, my heart racing.

"Demonstrators, workers from Wang Industries, are in front of the hotel. They are chanting slogans against Altéone and trying to attract attention. It's not an ordinary demonstration. We think they could try to breach security."

I was silent for a moment, trying to control the tension rising inside me. A demonstration in China, especially in front of a hotel like that, couldn't be a spontaneous occurrence. It was an orchestrated maneuver, with the tacit approval of influential authorities.

"Stay calm, François. I'll take care of it."

I went back to my seat and told Katrin that I had to leave.

"A problem at the office," I told her, trying to minimize the situation. "I'll send you a message later."

She raised her eyebrows but didn't ask any questions, respecting my need for discretion. I promised to meet her later at my suite, where she could wait for me.

As I left the arena, I quickly found my chauffeur, who was waiting for me with our American minivan, a faithful companion as I moved around in Shanghai. Once seated in the back, I told him, "The Ritz-Carlton. Quickly."

The journey was rapid and tense. I watched every movement through the vehicle's tinted windows, my mind already working to anticipate the next steps.

When I arrived at the hotel, I found a scene that was even more chaotic than I had imagined. A hundred or so demonstrators had gathered in front of the main entrance, brandishing placards that accused Altéone of "sabotaging the local economy" and "threatening Chinese workers." The slogans, carefully orchestrated, aimed to discredit us and send a message to local authorities.

I entered the hotel through a side entrance, guided by a member of security. In the lobby, Gabriel Lemoine was waiting for me, his expression somber and his glass of whiskey half-empty.

"It's staged," he said immediately. "Not just for us. They also want to show their strength to their allies."

"None of that can happen without political support," I replied, observing the scene through the window. "It's a war of influence."

We spent a good part of the night coming up with a response, while using our contacts to identify who was responsible. This demonstration was a clear message: Wang Industries and its allies intended to play all their cards, including those of alliances they had with the powers that be.

Night fell on Shanghai, and the Ritz-Carlton suite was apparently all calm. After a tense day marked with an orchestrated demonstration in front of the hotel and a date at the tennis tournament cut short, I had just got back to my room to try to get back some semblance of serenity. As planned, Katrin was waiting for me in the living room, holding a glass of white wine, a smile of complicity on her face.

"So, crisis resolved?" she asked, her light tone contrasting with the intensity of the day.

"Resolved? Nor really," I replied, smiling back at her. "But this evening, I'm just hoping for a break."

I quickly locked my computer, a gesture that had become a reflex, and I let myself sink into the sofa beside her. After a brief discussion punctuated by laughter and comfortable silences, we decided to go to bed for the night. The weight of the events of the day was crushing me, and sleep soon came to me.

At around three in the morning, a noise disturbed my sleep. A click, almost imperceptible, but enough to awaken my senses. I opened my eyes, looking around me in the semidarkness. Everything seemed calm. The blinking standby light on my computer was off, something odd that my still-foggy mind tried to rationalize. Tired, I fell back into a restless sleep.

It was only in the early morning, as the first rays of sun shone into the suite, that I realized that something was wrong. I went over to the desk to check my computer. The top was slightly open. My heart raced as I switched it on to check its content.

The "China" file, bait created to attract the attention of any intruders, had disappeared. Not moved, not modified – just erased. I went through the files, looking for a clue, but nothing. The computer seemed to be intact, other than this missing file. It was a clear message, "We can access your information, delete what we want, and leave without leaving a trace – even while you're sleeping."

I remained rigid, staring at the screen. This intrusion wasn't just an attempt at espionage. It was a declaration of power, a cold and calculated demonstration. The Chinese secret services, because it could only be them, had wanted to remind me of their omnipresence and their ability to act however they liked.

Katrin appeared in the doorway, still sleepy. "You're up already?" she asked me, yawning.

I smiled weakly, trying to hide my worry. "Just a bit of work," I replied. "Nothing urgent."

She nodded and went back to bed. I took a deep breath in, trying to control the anger and powerlessness I felt rising in me.

A few hours later, Gabriel Lemoine joined me in the suite. I quickly told him about the events of the night. He sat silently, frowning as I showed him the absence of the file.

"They didn't get anything," I said. "Nothing sensitive in any case. But they wanted me to know that they could come whenever they felt like it."

Lemoine nodded, pensive.

"It's not Wang Industries. It goes beyond that. An operation like this is straight from the authorities."

"They're trying to mess with our minds," I replied. "They know that we can't do anything against that, and they want to unsettle us."

"Well, don't give them that satisfaction," he replied firmly.

This intrusion confirmed that the war with Wang Industries wasn't just commercial or legal. It stretched into the shadows, involving state players ready to use their power to influence this conflict. That night, the agents hadn't just deleted a file. They had got rid of the illusion that my actions could go unnoticed in China.

The rest of the day was spent reinforcing our security systems. We doubled the protocols to protect our information, but deep down, I knew that it wouldn't be enough to stop such powerful players.

This intrusion, although disturbing, only strengthened my determination. If Wang Industries and their allies thought that these tactics would be enough to divert me from my objectives, they were underestimating my resilience.

As I watched the vibrant lights of Shanghai from my window again, I swore that that night would be a turning point. Wang Industries and their allies had crossed a line, and I was determined to respond, whatever it took.

After the intrusion into my suite at the Ritz-Carlton and the growing tensions around our mission, it seemed clear to me that staying in this hotel, as luxurious as it may be, was no longer a viable option. My movements were closely monitored, and every day spent there increased the risk of another incident.

So, I decided to move to the Shanghai Hilton, situated a few steps from the Xingye Center, where the regional head office of the Altéone Group in China was located. This choice was not just strategic, it also offered more discretion and a logistic proximity that was essential to manage this crisis.

The Shanghai Hilton, although less ostentatious than the Ritz-Carlton, was just as comfortable. Its spacious, modern rooms had clear views over the city, and its discreet service was perfect for my needs. I got settled in a suite on the top floor, a temporary but safe refuge, where I could coordinate our operations without attracting attention.

The proximity to the Xingye Center also simplified the daily meetings with Gabriel Lemoine and the Altéone team. The head office, situated in one of the most modern tower blocks in Shanghai, was a real nerve center for our operations in Asia. Every day, I could walk to our offices, crossing a busy street, blending in with the crowd of office workers and expats, thus escaping the surveillance that my travel by car often seemed to attract.

In spite of the change of hotel, the pressure didn't ease. In a few days, we noticed subtle signs that Wang Industries and their allies were still monitoring my movements. Unmarked cars seemed to park close to the Hilton at strategic times, and some faces kept appearing too often among the staff or visitors I met in the foyer.

To reinforce our security, Gabriel Lemoine hired a team that specialized in counter-surveillance, based in Singapore. These experts installed devices to interfere with any potential bugs in my suite and implemented strict protocols for our strategy meetings. We knew that Wang Industries and their allies in local power wouldn't back down from disrupting our efforts for anything.

At the Xingye Center, a secure room was procured for our most sensitive meetings. Inside, maps detailing Wang Industries' financial circuits hung on the walls, and statements of bank transactions and legal reports were piled up on the table in the middle of the room. Each detail was analyzed, each movement anticipated.

"We need to push them to make a mistake," I said one morning during a meeting with Gabriel Lemoine and the legal team. "They are strong, but their arrogance leaves them vulnerable."

One afternoon, as I was finishing a meeting with Lemoine, an influential Altéone local staff member, whom I had known for several years, asked to see me in private. His voice, which was usually assured, was cautious.

"They're trying to divide us," he said, placing an envelope on the table. "This was given to one of our local partners."

I opened the envelope and found a series of falsified documents, intended to make people believe that Altéone was involved in anti-competition practices in China. It was a clear attempt to sabotage our reputation with our local allies.

"We need to respond," he said, closing the envelope. "But without falling into their trap."

This new maneuver showed that Wang Industries was intensifying their efforts to isolate us. But every attack also strengthened my determination to respond.

The following days were marked by an intense, yet necessary, routine: meetings at the Xingye Center, phone calls with international lawyers, and strategy sessions to coordinate our movements. In spite of the constant pressure, the Hilton and the Xingye Center became an effective operational base, a place where I could work with a minimum of distractions.

The nights, however, were still difficult. Every noise in my suite, every shadow on the wall, brought me back to the intrusion at the Ritz-Carlton. But in those moments of doubt, I thought of the mission again. We weren't just there to protect Altéone's interests. We were there to show that, in spite of a hostile environment, it was possible to fight for the truth.

The move to the Shanghai Hilton, dictated by the need for discretion and proximity to the Xingye Center, also offered unexpected benefits. As well as giving me a comfortable, secure environment to pursue the mission, it marked the start of my relationship with the hotel chain. A relationship that, many years later, would lead to advantages that I had never imagined.

Every night spent at the Hilton added points to my loyalty account, without me paying attention to it. At the time, building up free nights or having a privileged status was the least of my worries. But over the months and many nights spent in the hotel chain, I reached Diamond status with Hilton Honors. This status, which I didn't know about at the time, would be one of the rare, pleasant bonuses of this tense period.

The Shanghai Hilton was a welcome refuge. Less exposed than the Ritz-Carlton, it offered the perfect balance between comfort and discretion.

The staff members, warm but professional, knew how to remain in the background, which meant that I could do my job in peace.

"Welcome, sir," the concierge would invariably say to me every evening as he greeted me, his sincere smile reinforcing the sense of normality that I desperately needed.

Breakfast served in the executive lounge, reserved for the most loyal clients, became a special time. In the morning, between two phone calls, I could enjoy a freshly prepared tea and a bowl of local noodles, a combination that gave me a rare feeling of stability in a context where everything felt uncertain.

It was only several years later that I realized how much those nights spent at the Shanghai Hilton changed my relationship with traveling. My Diamond status allowed me access to advantages that I would never have imagined: upgrades to suites, complimentary breakfasts, and above all complimentary nights in some of the most prestigious hotels in the world.

During last-minute trips or personal travel, I was able to enjoy hotels in exotic places – from the beaches of Thailand to the skyscrapers of New York – without paying a cent. Every time I settled into a luxurious suite or I woke up to a stunning view, I remembered the nights I spent in the Shanghai Hilton, where it all began.

Ironic, I often thought, that the most stressful moments of my career offered me opportunities for relaxation and discovery.

The Shanghai Hilton will always be etched in my memory as a place of intense work but also as a door opening onto experiences I could never have imagined. Every night spent there symbolized resisting the pressure of Wang Industries but also contained the promise of brighter days, when I would at last be able to enjoy the fruit of these efforts.

In spite of the constant tensions, the nervous meetings, and the shadows hanging over every decision, the Hilton became a special chapter in this battle. It was not just a place to sleep, it also represented an unexpected lesson: Even in the most complicated moments, unexpected benefits can emerge.

Hunting for the Truth Across the Americas

Shanghai was still bubbling with the tensions caused by the commercial and legal war between Altéone and Wang Industries, when Gabriel Lemoine suggested an audacious idea. During a strategy meeting at the Xingye Center, he set out his vision: to show that Mr. Wang, the man behind Wang Industries, was not as nationalist as he claimed.

"If he has a green card or if his family has ties with the United States, that could call into question his patriotic position," explained Lemoine. "That weakens his image and the support that he receives."

His reasoning was both brilliant and risky. If we could prove that Wang had significant interests outside China, that would undermine his credibility and strengthen our arguments, not only in the Chinese courts but also on the international scene.

Lemoine's idea opened a new option, but we needed to act quickly and covertly. I immediately offered to head up that mission.

"I'm ready to go," I said. "If we want to get results, we need someone who can navigate between cultures and between the different contacts."

Gabriel Lemoine accepted, and the plan was put in place. Before I went to the United States to track down evidence, first I needed to make a stopover in Mexico, where a security evaluation mission in a local Altéone unit awaited me.

At that time, I didn't yet know that Mexico would play a much more significant role in my life. A few years later, I would come back there to work on complex hostage-taking situations. These experiences, which were a mix of humanity and danger, would remain etched in my memory and play a decisive role in my career.

But at the time, my stop in Mexico was in a very different context: a security audit and an unexpected break in Cancún.

Landing in Mexico was a mixed experience. The airport, at the very heart of this sprawling megalopolis, offered a spectacular view over the never-ending lights of the city. But behind this luminous beauty, there was a feeling of insecurity hanging over everything. The violence of the cartels, although often invisible to foreigners, was nonetheless omnipresent.

I had two objectives in Mexico: to audit the security measures of the local Altéone unit and to prepare the next stages of my mission in the United States. The days I spent in this city were filled with visits to the offices, discussions with the security managers, and trips in armored SUVs to avoid high-risk areas.

Tension was constantly with me. Every journey reminded me that security, even when it is well orchestrated, is never a guarantee in such an unstable environment. Yet, in the middle of this chaos, I had a rare opportunity: to meet up with my best friend, Maja, a Croatian emigrant that I had met during my university years in Canada.

Maja, who worked at the Department of Health in Mexico at the time, had asked me to join her in Cancún for a few days. We had always been extremely close, and this reunion in a heavenly setting was a breath of fresh air in the middle of my professional obligations.

Cancún stood in striking contrast to the intensity of Mexico City. The beaches with turquoise sea, flaming sunsets, and the relaxed atmosphere allowed us to reminisce about our younger days in Canada. Between lively discussions and bursts of laughter, we talked about our respective paths and the choices that had brought us to where we were.

In spite of the beauty of this break, I kept in mind the mission ahead of me. Every moment spent in Cancún was also an opportunity to think about what was ahead and to plan my next moves in the United States.

After a few days of respite in Cancún with Maja, I headed off towards the heart of the mission. My next stop was Miami, a city filled with opulence and diversity but which also gave off a certain mystery. Under the bright sun and swaying palm trees, there was a hidden complex network of contacts and influencers. I wasn't there to enjoy the beaches or the lively evenings of South Beach, but rather to meet a key informer, a discreet man but one who was well-connected in immigration and American administration circles.

My arrival in Miami, under stifling heat, matched the tense atmosphere that had been with me since Shanghai. My contact, a man of around forty with an impassive face, had agreed to meet me in a modest coffee shop, far from the touristy areas of the city. The choice of place was deliberate: He was trying to avoid any prying eyes.

When I entered, I looked around the room, and he gave me a subtle sign from a table towards the back, his telephone placed face-down on the table. We exchanged a little small talk to break the ice, but he didn't take long to get to the point.

"Are you looking for information on anyone in particular?" he asked, taking a sip of black coffee.

"Mr. Wang," I replied calmly, so as not to attract the attention of the other customers. "You know what I want."

He nodded slowly, glancing briefly at the door.

"I can help you, but the real link is in San Francisco. There, you'll find someone who will be able to confirm to you all that you want to know. But be careful. What you're looking for is not easy to get. The people involved don't like us getting into their files."

The exchange was brief, almost clinical. He gave me a name and address in San Francisco, then stood up without waiting for me to finish my tea. His way of leaving, silent and effective, added to the tension. I know that what was ahead of me on the West Coast would be more complex.

Landing in San Francisco, I immediately felt that the stakes had just got higher. The city, surrounded by its usual morning fog, seemed colder and more distant than I remembered. I had chosen a hotel close to the airport for discretion, but it was only a temporary base. The key meeting was going to take place at the Westin, a very elegant hotel, situated in a strategically neutral area.

The local informer, whose name I had been given by my Miami contact, was a man known to navigate between the legal and the clandestine, using his knowledge of American administrative systems to supply sensitive information to those who could pay for it. He never appeared in person. Instead, he got his clients to follow precise instructions.

The first instruction was simple: depot off an envelope containing the agreed sum in a hotel room at a given time. In exchange, another envelope containing the documents would be left in this same room for me a few minutes later. A swift, effective procedure, but one that was not without risks.

On the day of the meeting, I went to the Westin with the envelope carefully tucked away in my bag. The immaculate hotel hallways were strangely silent, amplifying every sound of my steps. A surveillance camera blinked dimly in one corner, reminding me that in spite of the neutral appearance of the place, nothing went unnoticed.

The assigned room was on the third floor. I knocked gently at the door, but nobody answered. Following the instructions, I entered with the key that had been left at reception for me. The room was impeccable but impersonal, as if nobody had stayed there. The air had a slight smell of disinfectant, reinforcing the strange sensation that it was a place that was only used for specific purposes.

I set the envelope containing the money on a coffee table in the lounge near the window and then went back to the bedroom and sat on the edge of the bed, staring at the clock on the wall. The minutes dragged by. My mind played with possible scenarios: a scam, an intervention of the authorities, or worse, a trap set by allies of Wang Industries who could have anticipated my movements.

After exactly fifteen minutes, I stood up and opened the door to the living room to inspect the table. A second envelope, which was different from the first one, had been slipped under the decorative vase. My heart started racing as I took hold of it. Inside the envelope was a collection of documents, which had been carefully folded. My adrenaline spiked as I opened them.

The first lines confirmed to me what we suspected. Mr. Wang did indeed have a green card, and his daughter, who lived in the United States, had an American passport. The information included copies of official documents proving their status and details on the property registered in their names.

These discoveries were not just legal proof. They were strategic weapons. They highlighted an obvious contradiction in the nationalist position of Wang. This man, who was set up as the defender of Chinese heritage against foreign multinationals, had personally established solid roots on American territory.

I closed the envelope and stowed it carefully in my bag, before leaving the room. Every step until the hotel exit was filled with vigilance. I knew that I had just acquired crucial, but also possibly dangerous, information.

Once back at the airport, I took a moment to reflect on what we had achieved. This mission had been tense, every step weighed up carefully, but it was starting to bear fruit. Wang's green card was not just an administrative detail. It was a key to open new doors in our battle against Wang Industries.

As the plane took off, I thought that this success was just a step. The documents I was bringing back reinforced our position, but they would also attract reprisals. The war with Wang Industries was not going to calm down. It had just taken a new turn.

New York welcomed me with dark clouds, its avenues glistening under gentle rain that amplified the glow of the neon lights and the shop windows. Although this was a professional mission, it already had an almost cinematic aura. The city seemed to want to play a role in this complex intrigue.

Adam, my contact, was there to help me to find my way around this maze. As a former Kroll investigator, he was known for his discretion and his efficiency but also for his sharp personality, which couldn't abide delays. We had planned to start slowly, in an emblematic place that would allow us more to establish a foundation of trust than to get fully into the subject: the legendary Blue Note jazz club.

The Blue Note, nestled in the heart of Greenwich Village, was already busy when we got there. The air was heavy with animated conversations and captivating melodies. A singer with a deep voice was performing a Nina Simone classic, accompanied by a pianist, whose fingers seemed to dance over the ivory keys. This place was not just a club; it was a sanctuary where the history of jazz mixed with the contemporary intrigues of Manhattan.

Adam, dressed in a dark suit that was impeccably tailored, led me to a table over to the side, near the stage but isolated enough to allow us private conversation.

"Here, we talk about business to the rhythm," he said, with a half-smile. "The people you're looking for often pass through here. We listen, we learn, and if we're lucky, we get things to progress."

We ordered cocktails, but Adam remained vigilant, his gaze regularly sweeping the room. A few minutes later, he signaled to a man sitting nearby, who nodded, then when the song finished, came over to our table.

The man, whom I got to know under the name of Mr. Ching, was an enigmatic figure, clearly used to the subtleties of negotiation. He wore an impeccable suit and had a smile that didn't fully hide a certain caution. After a brief exchange of small talk, he soon got to the heart of the matter.

"Wang Industries has ties, but not where you think," he said in a low voice. "Chinatown is a front. The real influence is in the hands of a few discreet partners, and those partners are not only in legal business."

Adam nodded, and unsurprisingly, Mr. Ching went on. "If you are trying to understand their movements here, start with the Hong Kong connections. The Triads have more influence than you think."

He gave me a few names, avenues to explore, then got up briskly, bringing the conversation to a close. The exchange was brief but crucial, and it left me with a sensation of palpable tension.

As the music started up again, I tried to digest this information. The singer was giving a touching rendition of "Feeling Good," and for a moment, the weight of the mission disappeared, replaced by the raw emotion of the song. As for Adam, he seemed totally relaxed, sipping his drink as if it were an ordinary evening.

"You see," he said, smiling. "New York is like that. A song, a drink, and a piece of information can change everything."

I couldn't help but smile. He was right. This city had a unique way of combining the sublime with the pragmatic, the spectacular with the clandestine.

In the following days, Adam and I explored the avenues that Mr. Ching had given us. We spent hours wandering through Chinatown, going into shops and packed coffeehouses, listening to conversations and asking the right questions. Gradually, the contours of a complex network emerged: Wang Industries used a shell company based in Hong Kong to clandestinely finance its American operations. These connections also seemed to include partnerships with groups who had close ties with the Triads.

One afternoon, while we were sitting in a quiet little eatery, Adam made an observation that struck me.

"Those people," he said, pointing to a key figure we had just identified. "They never move without good reason. Every gesture has a purpose. If we follow them, we'll understand their plan."

After several days of intense investigation, Adam insisted on taking me to Madison Square Garden. He had courtside seats for a Knicks match, a luxury that contrasted with the tense atmosphere of the alleys of Chinatown.

The roar of the crowd, the raw energy of the game, and the shared camaraderie in the stadium gave me some welcome respite. For a few hours, I forgot my mission, letting myself get caught up in the adrenaline of the moment.

"You see?" Adam asked, with a smile at the corner of his mouth. "Even in this city, you need to take a break."

At the end of my mission in New York, Adam drove me to my hotel near Grand Central. Before leaving, he handed me a little black book full of names and numbers.

"These people," he said, tapping the notebook. "If you come back, they'll help you."

I thanked him, aware that this mission was only going to be one step in a much larger conflict. As I watched the city grow more distant through the window of the taxi that was taking me to the airport, I knew that New York had done more than just give me information. It had showed me that every city, every person can become an ally or an adversary in this shadow war.

The days I spent in New York were intense, marked by interesting encounters, promising avenues to explore, but also worrying shadow zones. The information gathered in the Blue Note and on the streets of Chinatown had revealed a complex network where the connections between Wang Industries, the shell companies based in Hong Kong, and figures associated with the Triads became more and more clear. However, this path, although intriguing, was also dangerous.

The Triads, with their reputation of being "merciless" and their transnational influence, represented a risk that I couldn't allow myself to take at that stage. Pursuing that avenue could have endangered not only my mission but the larger efforts that we were making against Wang Industries. After a conversation with Adam, we reached the same conclusion that we should redirect our efforts.

"You have what you need for now," Adam said, as he brought me back to my hotel. "But the Triads are a whole other level. You don't mess with them."

I nodded, aware that here caution was the best strategy. Rather than venturing further into a potentially explosive maze, I decided to fly to Los Angels, where other avenues were waiting to be explored.

Los Angeles was a different setting, but one that was every bit as strategic. This city, with its unique blend of cultures and its role as an international crossroads, represented an opportunity to carry on the investigation from a less risky angle, but one that was just as decisive.

As the plane took off from New York, I watched the lights of the city disappear over the horizon. New York had given me a fascinating and disturbing insight into the networks that Wang Industries had woven all over the world. But it was time to turn the page, to change scenes, and to carry on the battle in a new environment.

The American Dream

Los Angeles shimmered under the hot sun, but behind its glamourous appearance and its palm trees, there was a complex and risky mission: untangling Mr. Wang's possessions and assessing the scale of his activity in California. The Wang family, in spite of its public position, seemed to have woven a web of financial and real estate interests in the region. My work was to find them, to document them, and to provide them to lawyers as solid evidence for the upcoming lawsuit.

My partner in this mission was John, a local investigator with an inimitable style. Tall, with wide shoulders and a deep voice that seemed to shake the walls, John incarnated the perfect combination of efficiency and charisma. He mainly worked out of the Blue Ghost, an aging blue sedan that he used as a mobile office.

"Get in," he said, handing me a take-out tea. "The Blue Ghost will become your second office."

Inside the car was organized chaos: maps, laptop computers, files, and Post-it notes stuck everywhere. It was a hive of activity on wheels, where every journey turned into an opportunity to put information together.

When we weren't driving along the streets of Los Angeles, we worked out of the office that John shared with his brother, a local lawyer. That place felt like it was straight out of the 80s: dark wood walls, dull lighting, and piles of files that looked as though they had never been sorted. A secretary, clearly used to urgent tasks, calmly managed the surrounding turmoil.

"The charm of the old," John joked, pulling out a chair. "But this office has seen things, complicated cases."

It's here that we mapped the complex web of Wang Industries in California. The company, operating under another name, had properties hidden all over Los Angeles and the surrounding area. Each discovery, each link, added a piece to the puzzle.

The mission in Los Angeles was not just restricted to files and to meetings. It required hours of surveillance, tailing, and on-the-ground investigations that were often not very orthodox. John, with his sharp instincts, was a master in the art of tracking a target. Our work consisted of several types of actions:

- Discreet tails: We followed vehicles associated with the Wang family to identify their habits and localize their properties.

- Going through trash cans: By collecting documents carelessly thrown away, we found clues on the affiliates of Wang Industries and their financial transfers.

- Clandestine photos: We climbed fences to take photos of suspect properties, which were often luxurious and located in select residential areas.

- Telephone checks: Using databases, we traced calls from the affiliates' numbers to their local staff.

One afternoon, as we were tailing someone, we stopped at an In-N-Out Burger, an emblematic Californian fast-food chain. John was astounded to hear that I had never tried their hamburgers.

"Seriously?" he exclaimed. "You can't leave here without trying the best burger in the United States!"

Not only did he insist on buying me a full meal, but he also bought me a T-shirt with the inscription *In-N-Out Virgin!,* which he made me wear for the rest of the day. That lighthearted moment was a welcome break in a mission that required constant concentration.

Our efforts were starting to pay off. We identified several properties belonging directly or indirectly to the Wang family: grand houses in Beverly Hills, apartments in luxury buildings in Downtown LA, and even a ranch outside the city. The properties revealed a scale of assets that was much more significant than what we had initially estimated.

Wang Industries was also using shell companies to hide its transactions. Funds seemed to transit through offshore accounts before being reinjected into Californian projects. This information was crucial for our lawyers, because they showed a clear gap between the public statements of Wang and his real activities.

By also following members of the family, we got a better understanding of their habits and their local connections. That allowed us to map out a network that stretched far beyond Los Angeles, with potential ramifications all over the state.

One evening, as we were finishing up a long day in the Blue Ghost, John parked the car on a viewpoint overlooking Los Angeles. The lights of the city twinkled as far as the eye could see, an ocean of points of light in a dark sky.

"This city," he said, looking at the horizon. "It gives you everything and takes everything away. But if you know where to look, it doesn't keep anything hidden."

These words resonated with me. Los Angeles, with its contrasts and its excesses, was gradually revealing Wang Industries' secrets to us. But I knew that this battle, even if it was moving forward, wasn't over yet.

When the mission came to an end, we had compiled a critical mass of evidence. This information, combined with the results of the investigation we carried out in New York, gave our lawyers the necessary tools to put pressure on Wang and his empire. But this step was just one chapter in a war of influence that stretched across several continents.

Before taking me to the airport, John handed me a last In-N-Out T-shirt and, with his usual smile, said, "Keep that, my friend. You'll be back."

I left LA with a mixture of relief and determination. This mission had revealed some crucial truths, but I knew that the battle would go on and that I had other missions, elsewhere, ahead of me.

The mission in Los Angeles was intensifying when Alice and Annie, respectively Mr. Wang's daughter and his wife, left China for the United States. But other than their presence in California, one of the major objectives was to discover where exactly in China they lived. This information, which was essential for our lawyers, added a key geographic dimension to the case, by establishing links between their activities in China and abroad.

It's thanks to a precious source in the Chinese border patrols, developed over years, that I found out that they were leaving China. This source, infiltrated within the authorities, gave me information on the movements of persons of interest. They informed me that Alice and Annie had booked a United Airlines flight for San Francisco, a detail that got us to mobilize immediately.

Time was too short to organize surveillance right from their departure from China, so I concentrated on their arrival in the US. But this alert also confirmed to me a crucial hypothesis: They regularly used homes in China and abroad for their activities. Finding these properties became a priority.

From New York, where I was to take part in the General Assembly of the United Nations, I led this operation remotely with my BlackBerry, an essential tool to manage this mission of huge logistic complexity. The reports from the ground were coming through in real time, as I juggled between my diplomatic obligations and the meticulous monitoring of every movement in LA.

On their arrival in California, our surveillance teams took over. Once their localization was confirmed in a luxurious residence in Beverly Hills, we launched a detailed observation plan to map their movements and their routines.

Alice and Annie's residence, a manor nestled in an exclusive area, became the starting point for the operation. Six surveillance teams, or around fifteen agents, were deployed around the property and the itineraries they took regularly. Coordination was essential in order to remain discreet, while documenting every movement.

Their first stop was a high-end mall, where they spent several hours shopping. Then they headed to an exclusive spa/nail salon. This information, although it seemed simple, gave crucial clues to their habits and preferences, making further shadowing easier.

The key time during this operation was handing over a summons, a legal act that needed to be done directly, without ambiguity, in order to be valid. When they left the spa, one of the agents calmly approached them and handed the envelope to Alice. The reaction was immediate: Visibly irritated, she quickly read the document before contemptuously throwing it onto the ground. This scene was caught on video by our agents, thus ensuring proof of it having been officially handed over.

This gesture of defiance only strengthened our determination. It clearly showed that, in spite of their apparent flippancy, they were fully aware of the scope of the proceedings.

In parallel, thanks to my source at the Chinese border, I started to gather information on their residence in China. The aim was to confirm whether the properties identified matched those already associated with Mr. Wang or whether they revealed more ramifications to his empire.

This source also gave me details on the usual itineraries of Alice and Annie when they returned to China, in particular regular destinations in the exclusive residential areas of Huzhou. This information would be essential to widen the investigation on an international scale.

While the operation in Los Angeles came to an end, the information gathered revealed a clearer image of their network of residences and activities. Not only had we localized several of their properties in the US, but we were also starting to make connections between their assets in China and their international travel.

As I was leading this mission from New York, I also took advantage of the General Assembly of the UN to widen my network. Over the intense days, I met influential figures, including Paul Wolfowitz, a key person in diplomatic circles.

However, the combat was far from over. But every success, every piece of information brought us a little closer to the truth. And that, in a war of influence, was well worth the effort.

New York: An Encounter

That evening in New York, at the heart of the General Assembly of the United Nations, had a unique aura. My lawyer friend, who was working on the Wang Industries case, had organized a dinner for me with one of his friends, without telling me much about it. We were to meet at Socialista, a hip restaurant in the Meatpacking District.

When I arrived, she was already there, and she had an air of natural elegance. Alissa, the daughter of an influential east African president, a French ally, was wearing a perfectly tailored dress that showed off her silhouette and high heels that made her presence even more imposing. From the first moment, I was struck by her bearing but also by her smile and piercing gaze. We greeted each other and exchanged small talk, but soon the conversation became smooth, natural, as if we had known each other for years.

The dinner was delicious and animated. We talked about everything: our backgrounds, our travels, and our visions of the world. She was fascinating, combining charm and intelligence with disarming ease. But it wasn't just her beauty or her elegance that were captivating, it was her ability to talk with depth and sincerity.

After dinner, we decided to make an evening of it. That week, New York was unrecognizable. With the General Assembly taking place, roads that were usually teeming were deserted; many, like Park Avenue, Madison Avenue, and Fifth Avenue, were closed to traffic. That rare atmosphere gave us the impression that the city belonged to us.

We walked for hours, talking nonstop. Every street seemed to tell a different story, but that was what made this walk unforgettable. The clip of her heels on the silent sidewalks and the fluidity of her dress that danced lightly in the breeze added an almost cinematic touch to the night.

"New York is magical this week," she said, looking at the lights glowing all around us. "It feels even more beautiful like this."

Our walk took us to my hotel, near Grand Central Station. Neither of us wanted this unique evening to end. I invited her up, and she accepted without hesitation. My room, although modest, was spacious and had two beds. She chose one of them, but after a few moments, she joined me in mine. We were both exhausted from the long day, and without another word, we fell asleep almost instantly.

The next morning, she surprised me with an unexpected invitation. She was going to be celebrating her birthday in LA with her family, and she wanted me to join her before all headed off together for a weekend in Los Cabos, in Mexico. Her family would travel by private jet, but I would need to find a commercial flight. In spite of the unexpected nature of this invitation, I couldn't refuse.

The dinner, the walk, and the night in New York were the start of a relationship that would open up for me the doors to a world I could never have imagined. Alissa was not only fascinating, she was the link between several worlds: her African heritage, the international elite, and the excesses of a family whose power seemed to know no bounds.

Return to China: The Climax and the End of a Mission

My return to China coincided with an intense diplomatic period: the official visit of the French president, Nicolas Sarkozy. The tension was palpable. It wasn't just a battle between Altéone and Wang Industries but a diplomatic and legal war where every detail could influence relations between two major economic powers.

For me, it meant the conclusion of several years of investigations, shadowing, and constant research. I had gathered crucial information, exposed hidden connections, and supplied key elements to the legal teams. My role ended here. From now on, the conflict belonged to the diplomats and the lawyers, who were going to fight on playing fields where I could no longer intervene.

The arrival of Nicolas Sarkozy in China was strategic, marked by a willingness to reinforce Franco-Chinese relations. But this visit also added pressure to the Altéone-Wang Industries affair. China often used political leverage to support its national champions, and Wang Industries, under the leadership of Mr. Wang, had become a symbol of economic resistance in the face of multinationals.

In that context, my role was clear: to make sure that the information collected would serve as a solid foundation for the legal proceedings to come, while avoiding Altéone losing face diplomatically. Gabriel Lemoine, my boss, wanted everything to be perfect.

Back at the Xingye Center in Shanghai, I met Gabriel Lemoine for a decisive meeting. It was time to summarize years of work and to present the conclusions of my inquiries.

"We have everything we need," I told him, handing over a detailed report. "Properties in the United States, connections with the Triads, hidden activities through shell companies, and discrepancies in their statements."

Gabriel Lemoine briefly skimmed my documents. His face, usually impassive, betrayed a sense of satisfaction he was trying to hold back. We had gathered enough elements to strengthen Altéone's position, not only in the courts but also in the public arena.

"You have done a remarkable job," he said, closing the folder. "But from now on, it's a diplomatic and legal battle. The rest is up to the lawyers and the politicians."

I knew that he was right. My role, as critical as it may have been, ended here.

The next part would play out on two levels: legally, the American and Chinese lawyers would use the evidence gathered to expose Mr. Wang's contradictions and to strengthen the claims of the Altéone Group; in the area of diplomacy, the public relations teams and diplomats would work to limit damage to Franco-Chinese relations, while putting pressure on Wang Industries in a subtle yet effective way;

I was ready to intervene, if necessary, but I knew that a new phase of this conflict was beginning, a phase where my ground-level expertise no longer had a place.

As I left the meeting with Gabriel Lemoine, I took a moment to think back over those years of work. Ever since my first inquiries in Shanghai to the shadowing in LA and the meetings in New York, this mission had been one of the most complex and the most demanding of my career. It had allowed me to explore worlds that I didn't know, to work with unlikely allies, and to discover sometimes disturbing truths.

But it had also left its mark. The accumulated fatigue, the personal sacrifices, and the moments of constant tension had pushed me to my limits. But I knew that every minute had counted, every detail collected had served to build a strategy, which, I hoped, would give Altéone the advantage.

With Sarkozy's visit and the shift of this war onto diplomatic and legal ground, my mission came to an end. The combat, although far from over, was no longer mine. As I looked at the skyscrapers of Shanghai light up the night sky, I had a thought: Each conflict, however complex it may be, always ends up coming to an end.

I had a last drink at the Hilton, where I had spent so many nights planning, thinking, and analyzing. This city, with its contrasts and its challenges, would always be special to me. But it was time to turn the page and to prepare for my next mission.

Yet when I left China, I didn't know that one day I would be back to live through more adventures, which would be much more personal this time. Years later, I moved there again, as a witness and player in new chapters of my life, in particular the birth of my son. With hindsight, I see me leaving there in a totally different light: it was just a temporary goodbye, an au revoir to a land that still had a lot to offer me.

The Altéone-Wang Industries battle raged on for many more months, punctuated by legal and political developments. But my role was over.

This job, now finished, had marked a turning point in my career. It had taught me the importance of adaptability, patience, and perseverance, qualities that would accompany me on all my future missions.

As the plane took me away from China, I left behind me a little part of my story, without thinking that this land would one day call me back again to write a new chapter, one that would be more intimate – and deeper.

IV Shadowing Ricardo

First Mission in Indonesia

In 2007, when Ricardo, who was one of the greatest football players in the world, started a new phase of his career after his retirement from sport, he became a world ambassador for the image of an industrial company. For his first official visit to Indonesia, a country where the brand enjoyed huge popularity, the task I was entrusted with was exceptional: to ensure close security of Ricardo and his family.

At the time, Indonesia was facing latent instability. Terrorist threats, although few and far between, were very real, especially in large cities like Jakarta. My role consisted of orchestrating the whole mission: from logistics on the ground to coordination of local teams and anticipating all possible scenarios.

Arriving one week before Ricardo and his family, I knew that this mission involved unique risks. The JW Marriott Hotel, chosen as a backup plan for its proximity and its underground passage to the Ritz-Carlton, where Ricardo was due to stay, had a long history: It had just been rebuilt after being destroyed in a terrorist explosion in 2003. This event was still hanging in the air. The hotel staff were used to working under pressure, but the worried looks I saw showed acute awareness of the ongoing dangers.

Ironically, a few months after our visit, it would be the Ritz-Carlton itself that would undergo a similar attack, as if to remind us that the precautions we had taken hadn't been exaggerated. These facts reinforced how urgent my task was: protecting Ricardo, his family, and the team in an environment where the unpredictable is a fact of day-to-day life.

During those first few days, I spent a lot of my time training the drivers and the local security agents. Their initial skills were solid, but they needed to be adapted to the specific requirements of this mission. The training was on driving in a convoy, to make sure we would move around smoothly, even on the busy Jakarta roads; the evacuation protocols, simulating various scenarios, from mechanical breakdowns to medical emergencies; medical coordination, working with a local hospital to manage urgent journeys in the event of an injury or fainting; and navigation and reconnaissance of the places, which was crucial for identifying backup itineraries and avoiding the city's huge traffic jams.

Every day started with reconnaissance of the area: the winding roads of Java, with their frequent accidents, turned every journey into an unpredictable adventure, between the thick jungles and the stifling heat. In spite of these challenges, every site – whether it was a football ground or a presidential palace – was inspected centimeter by centimeter, documented in detailed sketches, and subjected to rigorous security tests.

The drivers, although used to the chaotic traffic of Jakarta, were surprised by the intensity of our training. One of them joked, "I thought I knew how to drive until today. Now, I think that I should take my driving test again!"

As I supervised these final adjustments to the security plan for Ricardo's visit to the presidential palace, an unexpected event occurred. Three men in uniform, introducing themselves as members of Paspampres (the Indonesian presidential guard), appeared in the office that I was using temporarily at the hotel. Their tone was both authoritative and insidious.

"Sir, your security plan for the palace has not yet received our final validation. You know that nothing can be confirmed without our agreement, and that could pose a problem… unless we can come to an agreement," one of the guys said to me with a forced smile.

The message was clear: They were hoping to extort money from me in exchange for validation, which, in reality, was already achieved. However, I was well prepared. I knew that the Indonesian president, Susilo Bambang Yudhoyono, was an unconditional fan of Ricardo's. He himself had insisted that the organization of this meeting was a priority.

Keeping my cool, I looked them straight in the eye.

"That's interesting, but I doubt that the president himself is aware of your demands. Maybe I should talk to him directly about it?"

Their smiles disappeared immediately. Without another word, they left the room. This episode, although irritating, was a reminder of the local power dynamics and the unexpected challenges that could arise even in very controlled environments.

These incidents only reinforced the importance of every detail. Every emergency exit, each camera, every journey between two places were checked, rechecked, and documented. My team and I simulated several scenarios, ranging from an intrusion attempt at the Ritz-Carlton to an emergency evacuation of the presidential palace.

The wasteland beside the Ritz was transformed into a helicopter landing zone, not without raising some protests from local children, used to playing football there. These adjustments, although logistical, were crucial to guarantee faultless security in an environment where the risks were everywhere.

One of the most demanding stages of this mission was reconnaissance of the isolated villages where Ricardo and his delegation were due to go for their charity work. These places, spread out in remote areas of Java, had to be secured to host the delegation and to guarantee their safety.

What would have taken an hour by helicopter turned into a several-day trip by car, through landscapes that were magnificent and unexpected. The use of helicopters for reconnaissance had been deemed too expensive, which forced us to use the winding roads of Java, where every kilometer seemed to bring its own challenge.

The journey, although exhausting, was also a constant source of wonder. We crossed rice paddies that shone in the sun, tea plantations that swayed to the rhythm of the wind, and dense tropical forests, where the light barely broke through.

The roads themselves were unpredictable: one minute they were asphalt, the next they became muddy tracks that were barely passable. The bridges suspended over raging rivers creaked under the weight of the vehicles, adding a dose of adrenaline to each crossing. But it was also this raw natural beauty that made the experience unique.

From time to time, we passed young Indonesian backpackers with smiles on their faces, exploring their own island with refreshing curiosity and a carefree attitude. They seemed surprised by our convoy but, always welcoming, they greeted us enthusiastically.

Each village we stopped in seemed to have its own character. The wooden houses, often decorated with traditional Javanese patterns, blended into the lush background. When we arrived, the inhabitants often came to meet us with curiosity mixed with kindness.

In a village nestled at the heart of the mountains, we were invited to share a meal under a large open hut. The dishes were simple but delicious: perfumed rice, fresh vegetables, and grilled fish served in a spicy sauce. It was over this meal that we chatted with the inhabitants, finding out about their way of life, their traditions, and their love for their land.

One of the elders, a man with a face marked by time, told us the story of his village and its bond with the surrounding nature. He explained that the tea plantations all around us had been farmed by his ancestors before him and that they were not only a source of revenue but also a symbol of harmony with nature.

These shared moments in the jungle became precious memories, contrasting strongly with the pressures and the logistics of the mission.

Because not everything was idyllic. The journey was physically demanding: Our days started at dawn and ended late in the night. The constant jolting of the drive on roads full of potholes made the tiredness palpable.

Added to that was the need to remain vigilant at all times. Each site needed to be meticulously inspected to anticipate the delegation's movements. We needed to identify the access points and the evacuation areas and even assess the resistance of the buildings against strong rains, which were frequent at that time of year.

In one particularly remote village, we had to come up with an evacuation plan in case of an emergency. The only path to leave the site went through a dense forest and crossed a river. It took us a full day to explore and map that journey, while finding solutions to reinforce the convoy's safety.

Each interaction with the inhabitants reminded us why this mission was particularly important. Ricardo, with his aura as world legend, was going to enter these villages not as an inaccessible celebrity but as an ambassador to a cause. And those moments brought us close to the communities that were going to welcome us.

In another village, a family invited us to their house for tea. The house, made from bamboo, was charmingly simple. The children watched us curiously, while the adults asked us questions about our work. At one point, an older woman addressed me directly, in a mixture of Indonesian and gestures: "Why are you doing all this for him? He is already so well-known."

After thinking for a minute, I replied, "Because his presence here could change lives. He gives hope, and it's an honor for us to protect that."

At night, when we got back to our modest accommodation or campsites after many hours of reconnaissance, we had time for silence and reflection. Once the teams had gone to sleep, I often allowed myself to go outside and look up at the sky, a pure sky that I had rarely seen elsewhere.

Without artificial lights, the stars shone with almost unreal intensity, lighting up the night sky in all its splendor. Familiar constellations and galaxies that we couldn't see in town revealed themselves to me, as if they wanted to remind me that, in spite of the challenges of this mission, there existed timeless, unchanging beauty in the universe.

These simple moments, where I stopped to observe, were filled with serenity. This sight captivated me, not only in Java but also later in other parts of the world. Even in more dramatic circumstances, where fear and uncertainty dominate, looking up at a starry sky always gives me hope.

I thought back to these moments afterwards, in less welcoming places, where the sky seemed to be my only ally. These stars were like a constant reminder that, however intense the mission or however tough the conditions, there is always a place, somewhere, where light persists, where chaos gives way to tranquility.

After days on end crisscrossing the roads of Java, through mountains, rice paddies, and tea plantations, the reconnaissance was coming to an end. We had inspected each place on Ricardo's itinerary, prepared evacuation plans, and coordinated with local teams. To celebrate the end of this crucial stage, we decided to give ourselves a night of relaxation in Jakarta, in a place that was much talked of at the time: the basement of the Shangri-La Hotel.

The Shangri-La, known for its luxury and its international clientele, had a nightclub in the basement, which was a hotspot for rich expats, influential businessmen, and the most elegant escorts in the country. It was a place where appearances matter and where, behind the smiles and laughter, the dynamics of power were at play.

That evening, the atmosphere was electric. Loud music, dim lighting, and boisterous laughter filled the space. Around us, there were tables of groups of men in suits, often accompanied by magnificently dressed women. Our little team settled in a corner, enjoying some relaxation after intense days of work.

Everything was going well until an expat who had clearly had too much to drink started provoking a group of Indonesian men at a neighboring table. The shouts soon rose. In this kind of place, where egos are as big as the fortunes, often it only takes a spark to enflame a situation. And that's what happened.

A fight broke out, chairs were knocked over, glasses broken, and insults fired off in several languages. The situation quickly became chaotic. Clients tried to take cover, while others got involved in the conflict.

I knew that getting involved in a situation like this, even just as a spectator, could have disastrous consequences, especially the day before Ricardo arrived. So, while the club's security tried to calm down the situation, I looked for an exit.

That was when I bumped into Steve, a former British military man I had met in Nigeria a few years earlier. Steve, a regular here, had an almost encyclopedic knowledge of the discreet exits and the "right way to go about things" in order to avoid issues in a country where corruption and connections were often necessary so as not to have any problems.

"Follow me, mate. This kind of bloody mess always ends badly," he told me, grabbing my arm.

We took a service corridor, going through the Shangri-La's kitchens and nearly missing a confrontation with the police, who were already arriving in force to get the situation under control.

Once we were outside, Steve, true to his British humor, burst out laughing.

"Welcome to Jakarta. First rule here: Never stay too long in a club where the expats are drunker than the locals."

I couldn't help but laugh. That evening, although chaotic, was a reminder of how important it is to remain vigilant in all circumstances, even during moments of relaxation. Remain grounded, never lose sight of the main objective, whatever the distractions or unforeseen incidents.

After that adventure, I went back to the hotel late in the night, still shaken by what had happened. As I was sitting near the window of my room, looking out over the twinkling lights of Jakarta, I realized how every moment counted in this job. The mission was about to enter its most critical phase, and there would be no room for improvisation now.

On the day when Ricardo and his family were to arrive, the atmosphere was filled with palpable tension. At Soekarno-Hatta international airport, journalists, fans, and the curious had gathered around the barriers, hoping to catch a glimpse of the man they thought of as a living legend.

The welcome plan, meticulously designed, required perfect coordination. A team of local motorcycle riders opened the way to clear the roads, while a convoy was waiting on the tarmac, ready to leave as soon as Ricardo and his family disembarked from the plane. It was at that moment that a key person in the mission appeared: Samir, Ricardo's imposing bodyguard.

But Samir was much more than just a bodyguard. This man, of North African origin, had an impressive presence with his massive frame and his piercing gaze. When he worked for the company that Ricardo represented, he became Ricardo's shadow, watching over him with unfailing loyalty. Outside of these missions, Samir had a much more modest job: He was head of security at the company's Paris headquarters' reception. But under the apparent simplicity was an extremely skilled man.

Furthermore, behind his intimidating physique, Samir was known for his disarming kindness, a rare quality in this field. Always respectful and thoughtful, he inspired both confidence and fear, because he also knew how to be firm when the situation required it. His presence at the airport that day was a relief for me. As I saw him heading up the first checks and managing the movements around Ricardo with military precision, I knew that we were in good hands.

After getting them settled at the Jakarta Ritz-Carlton, and on a relatively calm night, the mission began its first official visit: to a school situated in an isolated village at the heart of the island of Java. This event marked the start of Ricardo's humanitarian work in the area, an initiative meant to strengthen the image of the company he was the face of, while supporting local causes.

The journey, although it was short by helicopter – around one hour – was a real logistical challenge. Three crafts were used to transport the delegation: Ricardo and his family in the first one, while Samir and I were with the security teams in the two others. At every step, the procedures were meticulously followed: equipment checks, a briefing with the pilots, and visual reconnaissance of the landing areas.

Arriving was spectacular. The helicopter threw up clouds of red dust that surrounded the landing zone. The inhabitants, already gathered around the perimeter, called to Ricardo as soon as he got out of the vehicle. Their enthusiasm was palpable, but the crowd, although friendly, had to be carefully managed.

The school was a few hundred meters from the landing zone, nestled between the terraced rice fields and the green hills. A simple yet robust structure, with white limewashed walls and a tin roof, it was decorated with colored drawings by the children. The students, dressed in neat school uniforms in spite of the heat, were patiently waiting for Ricard to arrive.

As soon as he walked through the door of the school, they rushed towards him, holding out flowers and drawings for him. Ricardo, true to form, bent down to their height, listening attentively to their shy words.

One of the most touching moments took place when he improvised a little football match in the dusty schoolyard. We only had a worn leather ball, but the children's enthusiasm and Ricardo's dexterity transformed the moment into a memorable experience.

"He could play with anyone, but right now he's playing as if it were the World Cup Final," murmured Samir, his arms crossed, watching the crowd.

That moment, although simple, reflected the essence of Ricardo: a man who was able to use his talent to bring people together and inspire them, even in the most remote places.

As we were getting ready to return to Jakarta, a minor incident almost disrupted the mission. A group of adults tried to breach the security perimeter to get closer to Ricardo, hoping to give him letters and gifts. Although their intentions were obviously friendly, the situation could have quickly degenerated.

Thanks to rapid coordination with the local agents, the situation was calmed down without any major incident. Ricardo himself insisted that the letters were accepted and read later. This gesture, although small, showed his respect for the people who admired him.

Once back in Jakarta, the delegation prepared for the second major stage of the mission: a meeting with the Indonesian president, Susilo Bambang Yudhoyono, in the presidential palace. This ceremonial event had its own challenges with regard to security.

The palace, a majestic building surrounded by lush gardens, teemed with guards and journalists. In spite of appearances, the protocol was strict, and every member of the team had to comply with local directives. Samir supervised the final adjustments, making sure that the convoy was ready to leave at any time.

President Yudhoyono greeted Ricardo with visible enthusiasm, almost like a fan. After the official greetings, the conversation became more relaxed. Yudhoyono, known for his love of football, confessed that he had followed every match of Ricardo's during the 1998 World Cup.

"You are a source of inspiration to my people," he declared, giving Ricardo a firm handshake.

This meeting ended with the symbolic gift of a football shirt signed by Ricardo, a gesture that delighted the president.

The next day, another key stage of this mission was the parade in the streets of Jakarta, organized in collaboration with the city's mayor. The event, although it looked festive, had political implications: It came right around the time of the municipal elections, and Ricardo's presence, as a true international icon, added some sparkle to the mayor's campaign.

The scene was spectacular. The streets of Jakarta, usually jammed with vehicles, had been partially closed to allow the parade to cross the city. A huge crowd lined the roads, brandishing flags, signs, and balloons in the city's colors. Chants, cheers, and shouts of "Ricardo!" rang out in the warm, humid air of the afternoon.

Ricardo and the mayor were standing in the front of an open-topped Jeep, waving to the crowd. Behind them, Samir and I were standing in the back of the vehicle, trying as well as we could to hold on to the metal structure while surveilling the surroundings. It was not a comfortable position, but it was the best way to get an overview of the crowd and to intervene rapidly if there was a problem.

The logistical challenges were huge. The crowd, although joyous, represented a constant risk. People tried to get approach the Jeep, sometimes running alongside the vehicle or reaching out objects to Ricardo for him to sign.

Behind us, a Toyota Land Cruiser transported the rest of my security team. The agents, standing on the running boards or hanging on to the vehicles doorframes, maintained constant vigilance. This kind of vehicle was not chosen randomly. Toyota Land Cruisers have been my vehicle of choice for years, with me on the most demanding missions all over the world.

Land Cruisers are much more than just a means of transport. They are a symbol of reliability and sturdiness in extreme conditions. Whatever the terrain – arid deserts, tropical jungles, snowy mountains, or conflict zones – these vehicles have always got the job done. With unrivaled robustness, they are capable of crossing rivers, climbing steep slopes, or driving on potholed roads with ease. Moreover, their adaptability is impressive: The ability to modify them (reinforced seats, compartments to store equipment, and sometimes even light armor plating) makes them the ideal vehicle for security. Finally, although they are imposing, they are still common vehicles in many regions, which means that you can blend into the background with them.

In this mission, as in so many others, Land Cruisers were the backbone of our convoy. They also transported essential equipment, gave a raised position to observe the crowd, and guaranteed quick evacuation if necessary.

As the parade moved through the streets, a moment of tension occurred. A man, clearly excited by the event, tried to push through the crowd to approach the Jeep. Samir, ever attentive, noticed him right away.

"Careful on the left," he murmured, indicating the man by tipping his chin.

In a few seconds, I jumped down from the Jeep to intercept the individual before he could reach the vehicle. The man, although he wasn't threatening, was carrying a backpack, which needed to be checked quickly. Fortunately, he was just an enthusiastic fan who wanted to give a gift to Ricardo.

As I mentioned, beyond the festive atmosphere, this parade also had a political dimension to it. The mayor, a charismatic, calculating man, was obviously trying to use the event to strengthen his image. Every time the crowd cheered Ricardo, he made sure he was by his side, waving and smiling as if he shared a private connection with the champion.

At one stage, the mayor turned to Ricardo and said, "You know, your presence here is worth more than ten campaign speeches. The people love you."

Ricardo simply replied with a smile, avoiding any political comment.

When the parade reached its destination, a large square in the center of Jakarta, the crowd was even denser. Ricardo stepped up to a platform to briefly address the inhabitants, expressing his gratitude for their warm welcome.

During that time, Samir and I remained alert, scrutinizing the faces in the crowd, anticipating any suspect movements. Once the speech was over, we helped Ricardo to get back into the Jeep, and the convoy moved off slowly, leaving a euphoric crowd behind.

This parade was a key moment of the mission, not only for Ricardo's visibility and that of the company, but also for the unique experience that it gave the people of Jakarta. For me, it reinforced an essential truth: The logistics and the security of an event on this scale are often a matter of planning and adapting when on the ground.

And as is often the case, it was the Land Cruiser, that faithful companion, that allowed us to get through that eventful day successfully.

The mission was coming to an end with almost ceremonial discretion. After the parade and the last official events, Ricardo and his family were driven to the Soekarno-Hatta international airport for their flight back. It wasn't a private jet this time but a commercial flight with the Indonesian national carrier, Garuda Indonesia, in business class. This choice, typical of Ricardo, showed a simplicity that was almost unsettling for a personality of his status.

For the last time, the convoy slowly crossed the busy Jakarta streets. The city, still as chaotic and vibrant, seemed to be cheering Ricardo in its own way. The atmosphere in the vehicle was calm. Ricardo, as usual, didn't talk, concentrating on his thoughts or maybe just tired from the intense days he had just had.

At the airport, the procedures were as inconspicuous as possible. A VIP lounge had been set aside for Ricardo and his family, but the departure was marked by total simplicity. Ricardo, holding his two children by the hand, was silent, as his wife, Catherine, oversaw the final preparations for boarding.

On the tarmac, at the time of boarding, Ricardo finally turned to me.

"Thank you," he said simply, his expression sincere, but with the reserve that is typical of him.

Those were the only words he addressed to me throughout the whole mission. But in that brief exchange, there was clear recognition: The mission had gone without a hitch, and that was all that mattered.

Ricardo, Catherine, and their children, Hugo and Mathis, boarded the plane that would take them to Bali, where they were taking a well-deserved holiday. Ricardo often used his official trips to combine work and family time, giving his family the chance to discover the world by his side.

Ricardo's children, who were curious and lively, would become central figures in my life in the following months. I would spend a lot of time by their side, getting to know better the dynamics of this unique family and the outward-looking upbringing that Ricardo gave them.

As the Garuda Indonesia plane sped down the runway, ready to take off, I stood back, watching the moment with a mixture of satisfaction and relief. The mission had gone without any major incidents. But above and beyond the results, it had been special in a lot of ways.

Ricardo, in spite of his status as a legend, remained an enigma. He hadn't tried to make conversation or create a personal bond with me, but that silence was part of his character: reserved, humble, and focused on what mattered. He didn't need words to express who he was: His attitude and his gestures spoke for him.

What I didn't yet know at the time was that Ricardo had an extremely restricted circle and that he opened up to very few people. It wasn't a question of arrogance or coldness but a way of maintaining his balance and his peace of mind in a world where everyone wanted a piece of him. Over time, I would find out that he carefully chose the people he trusted and that there weren't many people who had this rare privilege.

What I didn't know either was that that first "thank you," although simple, would mark the start of a bond that would strengthen in future months and years. Ricardo would gradually open up the doors to his circle to me, entrusting me with responsibilities that I couldn't yet begin to imagine. But at that very moment, I was just a silent link in a mission that had gone to plan.

That mission had taught me a new lesson: The success of a mission doesn't rest on thanks or praise but on its smoothness and efficiency. If Ricardo, Catherine, and their children were able to enjoy their trip to Bali with total serenity, then my role had been fulfilled.

Egypt: Between Personal Holidays and Protocol

Egypt, with its mythical landscapes and its antiques treasures, offered an exceptional setting for this particular mission. But between the splendor of the pyramids and the mystery of the Sphinx, my role went far beyond just security. This mission, divided into two parts, combined close protection and the organization of an official visit, all in a country where the cultural and political aspects required constant vigilance.

As soon as we arrived in Cairo, the team and I began a meticulous assessment of the accommodation options for Ricardo and his family. We appeared to have two main choices: the Grand Hyatt and the Four Seasons, two prestigious hotels situated close to each other.

The Hyatt had an undeniable advantage: a private elevator – reserved solely for the hotel owner, a rich Gulf magnate – for discreet access to a private suite. That level of discretion and security was rare, and I was convinced that it was the ideal option. But Catherine, Ricardo's wife, preferred the spa at the Four Seasons, known for its excellence. We had to juggle between the two sites, which involved regularly escorting Catherine to her haven of relaxation, while the children made do with the Hyatt's pool. It was often me who took them, guaranteeing their security while making sure they had fun.

The days were punctuated by activities that combined relaxation and discovery. Ricardo, as was his style, wanted to offer his family a memorable experience. One of the best moments was a private visit to the Cairo Museum, where the children ran around between the sarcophagi while Ricardo, clearly fascinated, chatted with the curator of the treasures of Tutankhamun.

An excursion into the desert on horseback, near the pyramids, was also planned. The golden sand, lit by the setting sun, created an almost unreal atmosphere. We had hired an exceptional guide: Zahi Hawass, the most well-known Egyptologist in the country, known all over the world for his archeological discoveries. Nicknamed "Indiana Jones" for his appearance and his passion, he told stories of the Pharaohs earnestly, transforming every stone, every sand dune into a door that opened onto a fascinating past.

Later, always prepared to improvise a match anywhere, Ricardo proudly posed for photos with his children at the foot of the Sphinx, holding a football.

Every moment was a reminder of how he tried to maintain a balance between his private and his public life, a balance that we were there to protect.

Egypt is a country where chaos seems to reign, especially on the roads of Cairo. Driving there is an anarchic ballet, with cars everywhere, constant horns, and pedestrians that flaunt the rules and cross anywhere. During one of our journeys in an official convoy, this chaos took a dramatic turn.

We were being escorted by Egyptian police outriders and a special close protection unit. Their work was to secure the journey, clear traffic, and make sure that we reached our destination without a hitch. But that day, the reality on the ground got ahead of the organization.

As the convoy was moving slowly through a traffic jam, one of the outriders, while trying to avoid a vehicle, was hit hard by a car. The driver, without even slowing down, carried on, leaving the seriously injured policeman lying on the ground.

The convoy stopped immediately. Samir and I got out of the car right away to help. The motorbike rider, who was lying on the ground moaning, was bleeding abundantly. As we got closer, we realized with horror that he had lost two fingers in the accident.

Without wasting any time, Samir, with his usual cool head, picked up the amputated fingers and tried to put them back in place. In a succession of rapid, precise gestures, he wrapped the hand in an improvised bandage, trying to limit the damage until the emergency services arrived. The rider, although in shock, remained conscious, but it was clear that he was in pain.

A few minutes later, other police arrived to look after their injured colleague. We got back into the car, the convoy moved on, and the mission carried on as if nothing had happened. But in the vehicle, there was a weighty silence. This incident was a brutal reminder of how fragile our lives are, even in the context of a perfectly organized journey.

The high point of this mission was a lavish reception that took place in front of the majestic pyramids of Giza. The event brought together influential Egyptian personalities and international guests. Escorting Ricardo to his table, I made sure that everything was okay before joining a nearby table with his children, Hugo, Mathis, and Tom. But soon a little logistical issue arose: We were missing a chair for Tom.

Seeing an unoccupied chair at a neighboring table, I took it without hesitating, and the watching waiters didn't say anything. I thought that that was the end of the matter. But thirty minutes later, the atmosphere changed. An Egyptian minister arrived with great pomp, greeting the assembly before sitting down... or trying to. Just then, I saw a waiter whispering to him and pointing to me.

The minister, clearly furious, came towards me and started shouting at me in Arabic. No doubt thinking that I was just a member of the local protection team, he pulled no punches.

I tried to remain calm, but before I could reply, Ricardo intervened. His presence alone was enough to make the minister change his tone, realizing his mistake and apologizing with obvious hypocrisy. This altercation, although quickly defused, reminded me of an essential fact: Managing egos and protocols is as important as managing physical risks.

Later in the evening, as the lights illuminated the pyramids and the air was filled with a mixture of excitement and music, Mathis, the youngest of Ricardo's children, asked me a question that caught me off guard,

"Why does everyone want to be with Daddy? Why do they never let us be?"

I looked around me, hoping that someone would help me. Samir, who knew the children well, looked down at his plate. Matthieu, another member of the team, did the same thing. I realized that they weren't going to help me out.

Taking a deep breath in, I crouched down to his level.

"You know, Mathis, your dad is an inspiration for a lot of people. He gives them hope; he makes them happy. That's why they always want to be near him."

Mathis appeared to think for a minute, staring at an invisible point. I felt that he wasn't entirely satisfied with my answer, but before he could ask another question, I decided to distract him.

"Do you want to play football?"

His face lit up immediately. With Ricardo, football was a constant. Whether it was in a plane, a restaurant, or even here, there was always a ball around.

In a moment, the children forgot their worries, and we went outside, improvising a little match under the stars, with the pyramids in the background.

Egypt, with its captivating scenery and its unique blend of modernity and ancestral traditions, never failed to surprise me. Every day brought its share of intense, often unexpected experiences, which transformed this trip into an adventure that went beyond just a security mission.

One of the most memorable moments of this mission started in a completely ordinary way. One evening, when everyone was in bed, one of the trip organizers, a member of the company communications agency, invited me to go out, an informal invitation from one of the trip's cameramen. After several busy days supervising every detail of Ricardo and his family's security, the idea of relaxing a little was tempting.

"Okay, it will do us good. Just for an hour or two," he said to me, with contagious enthusiasm.

Without thinking too much, we got into a car, looking forward to enjoying a lighthearted moment. But very soon, the atmosphere changed. The car left the lights of the city and headed into the darkness of the desert. One hour passed, then another. With each kilometer, my worry increased. All around us, there was nothing but sand dunes and an oppressive silence.

I was starting to think that we had made a monumental error. Every possible catastrophe scenario ran through my mind. I glanced over at my companion, who also seemed to be getting more and more nervous.

"I'm not feeling it... We're going to end up on TV, our heads chopped off," I said half-seriously, half-humorously to lighten the tension.

But just when the panic was about to set in for real, an unexpected sound rang out in the desert air.

Music. Then lights, more and more visible, and at last, a row of palm trees appeared on the horizon. It was an oasis, and in the middle, an unlikely rave party was going on.

The atmosphere was electric: Young people were dancing under the stars, DJs were playing techno music. For several hours, we were transported to another world, forgetting the stress and the pressure of our responsibilities.

We got back in the wee small hours of the morning, exhausted but still astonished by this surreal experience. Unfortunately, there was no respite in store. We had only just got back to the hotel, when I realized that we had a meeting with Ricardo, the CEO of the company he was the face of, and the delegation from this company to visit factories located two hours from Cairo.

The journey in the convoy was torture. My eyes kept closing in spite of me, and at one stage, I gave in to the fatigue. In cars, my instructions were clear: Nobody should open the doors or get out of the car without my authorization. This strict protocol ensured the safety of the whole convoy. So, when we reached the site at last, everyone was waiting for me to give the signal to get out. But, fast asleep, I didn't move. After waiting for ten minutes, the CEO, exasperated by the delay, got out of his car and walked quickly towards my vehicle. Then he knocked loudly on my window.

The noise woke me up with a start, and I understood right away that I had made a mistake. I rolled down the window, still sleepy, and I saw the angry expression on the CEO's face. Without saying a word, he turned around and went back to the others, leaving us in an awkward silence. It wasn't my best moment.

This anecdote, although slightly embarrassing, demonstrates that in this job, tiredness is a silent enemy. Every detail counts; every second of inattention can have consequences. But it was also a lesson in humility, a reminder that even the best-prepared professionals are only human.

During this trip, I spent a lot of time with Ricardo's children, especially Hugo and Mathis. Ricardo always had a football handy. It was almost an extension of his person, a tool that allowed him to create bonds, to have fun, and just to be himself, even outside of football grounds.

With his children, he started football matches everywhere: in hotel corridors, on the terrace, or even by the swimming pool. However, I soon noticed that Mathis, unlike Hugo, didn't have the same skill for games involving the feet. He preferred holding the ball in his hand, squeezing it like a precious treasure, rather than dribbling it or kicking it.

Ricardo, who loved to gently tease the people around him, often made fun of this habit. And I often amused him with my own comments.

"Leave your son alone, Ricardo," I joked. "You can see that he doesn't want to play football like you. Look, he holds the ball like a basketball player. Maybe he'll end up in the NBA rather than becoming a footballer."

These light moments made Ricardo laugh, as he enjoyed this good-natured teasing. But looking back on it, I realize that my comments weren't so far off the mark: Mathis ended up becoming a goalkeeper, a role where you use your hands more than your feet. Even when he was young, he already showed that preference, a sort of natural instinct that would become his sporting future.

At the end of the day, this trip was a patchwork of contrasted moments, where the serious side of responsibilities mixed with moments of lightness and surprise, like that impromptu football match under the pyramids or the improbable rave party in the middle of the desert. But in all these experiences, one thing remained constant: the duty of protecting Ricardo and his family and making sure that, within this organized chaos, everything went according to plan.

Poland: Between Discipline and Improvisation

The icy air of Poznań even got under my bodywarmer. I had just spent a week preparing this mission in one of the most impressive places I have ever seen: the European Security Academy. Tucked away in the Polish countryside, this former farm, transformed into an elite training center, looked like a playground for professionals in the field of danger. It had everything: ultramodern shooting ranges, a miniature town to simulate urban combat, armored vehicles, and even a helicopter.

Dr. Bryl, the academy director, was an impressive person. Tall, calm, and with almost intimidating wisdom, he commanded respect as soon as he entered a room. His son Bart, with whom I soon forged a friendship, shared the same passion for close protection. Together, we had spent hours working on advance prep: reconnaissance of places, identification of evacuation routes, risk analysis. But these preparation days weren't just done seriously. The evenings in the old farm, with traditional Polish dishes and lively discussions, had created a rare camaraderie.

One of the agents from the local team had particularly attracted my attention. He was huge in the Polish special forces, always impeccable, and he kept a precious photo in his wallet: himself in uniform, beside Pope John Paul II. He had explained to me in hesitant English how much this blessing has marked his life.

It was our third night on the farm. I had just shut my eyes after a long day of preparation when Bart, the son of Dr. Bryl, knocked on my door.

"Come, my father wants to see you," he said, with an enigmatic smile on his face. I followed him, intrigued, down to the farm's basement, where there was an underground shooting range.

The place was both spartan and impressive. The walls resonated with heavy silence, only broken by the metallic sound of the targets moving. Bart handed me a Glock 19, giving me a knowing look.

Dr. Bryl was standing in a corner, with his arms crossed. "We're going to do a shooting exercise," he said calmly, but his tone told me that this wasn't going to be an ordinary session.

Then I asked, "What about the ear protectors?"

Dr. Bryl turned to Bart and answered with a seriousness that struck me, "In real life, in a shooting, you won't have ear protection. If you want to survive, you need to train as if it were in combat."

Bart turned on a stereo system that pumped out deafening hard rock music. Then, with a swift gesture, he switched out all the lights. The range was plunged into total darkness, only broken by the violent purple lights simulating explosions.

"Here is the scenario: You need to shoot the *bad guy* without hitting the hostage. And remember, chaos is your only point of reference."

The first shot made me jump, but I didn't have time to think. The targets sprang up out of nowhere, at improbable angles, sometimes with bright flashes or sudden noises. Every shot rang out like a jackhammer in my uncovered ears.

The music was so loud that my thoughts were drowned in the commotion, but my instinct came out on top. I just focused on the essential things: distinguishing between the enemy and the hostage, aiming, firing.

The session lasted forever. My heart was beating hard, my hands were sticky, and my ears ringing already. When the lights came on at last, Dr. Bryl came over, a little smile on his face.

"Well done," he said simply. "You hit all the enemy targets. But more importantly, you kept calm. That is what will save you, not your ears."

My ears rang for a week after that session. Maybe I lost a little bit of my hearing that night, but deep down, I understood that this training might save my life one day.

On the big day, everything was ready. The private jet with Ricardo and the CEO of the company he was the face of landed on the tarmac of the private terminal of Poznań in the early afternoon. The arrival was simple yet elegant. Ricardo, as always, disembarked the plane with a relaxed walk, while the CEO was already talking about logistics with his assistant. The local agents were lined up in formation, professional and focused.

The first few hours of the mission went without a hitch. The events that were to take place in Poznań were well-organized and blended cultural visits and promotional work for the company. Ricardo shone with his simplicity and kindness, taking the time to greet everyone, from officials to children who had come to see him.

The journey to Warsaw created a different atmosphere. The Polish capital, which was having a renaissance after entering the European Union, had two sides to it: that of a modern city that wanted to rival other European capitals, and the side made up of areas marked by visible scars of the Second World War. Ricardo and the CEO, along with their delegation, were welcomed to this place where history could be seen on every building. One of the most striking moments was a visit to a poor neighborhood where the bullet marks on the walls still told of the past horror.

One of the many events organized for this mission was a visit to the Poznań stadium, and it was no doubt the most memorable. The day was dedicated to children, and Ricardo was to lead a football session for young people from the region, who came from disadvantaged areas.

As soon as he came onto the pitch, the energy changed. Ricardo had a unique gift of elevating an ordinary meeting to the level of a magical moment. As soon as he was with the children, everything felt natural. He spoke to them gently and simply, giving technical advice on their dribbling or passing but also sincere encouragement about their dreams.

At one stage, a boy of around eight years old was struggling to follow his instructions. Ricardo went over to him, crouched down to his level, and said something to him in French. The child, who probably didn't understand what he had said, answered with a shy smile, but that interaction was enough to give him back his confidence. A few minutes later, he scored a goal, and Ricardo ran over to him to celebrate with him as if it were a World Cup Final.

The joy that Ricardo expressed in these moments was palpable. It wasn't just a promotional task for him. He liked being there, with children, sharing his passion for football and giving them tangible hope.

"Ricardo doesn't do this for the money," Samir murmured beside me. "It's in his DNA. Teaching, inspiring... that's who he is."

Watching Ricardo evolve like that gave me another perspective on him. He wasn't just a champion but a man who was driven by a larger mission.

He didn't just see children, he saw a future generation he could inspire with passion, a love for the game, and self-confidence.

On the last day, everything seemed to be going according to plan. Ricardo and the CEO were due to leave for Madrid after a series of successful events. The convoy was in place, the vehicles ready, the itineraries verified. We were driving in convoy along the narrow streets of Poznań towards the airport's private terminal, when suddenly something came through the radio.

"Alpha One, why are you speeding up?" I asked, my tone already giving away some concern.

It was silent for a few seconds, then the deep voice of the agent in the lead car answered, "Ricardo is late for Madrid. He has asked us to speed up."

I gritted my teeth. Protocol requires the convoy to remain tight. Uncontrolled acceleration could compromise the whole group's safety.

"Slow down immediately. We can't take any risks," I ordered firmly.

But Ricardo's car kept on getting further in front. Without thinking, I raised my voice. "Alpha One, slow down, now!"

No response. The situation was rapidly degenerating into chaos. My driver, a young man from the local team, turned to me, awaiting my orders.

"Follow them, but keep your distance," I told him, short of breath.

What came next was like something out of an action movie. The convoy drove through the streets of Poznań at top speed, the tires screeching over the cobbles. Passersby hurriedly moved out of the way, surprised by the sudden nature of this race through their usually quiet town.

I glanced at my watch: every second counted. Ricardo needed to be in Madrid for a key event, and there was no way he could miss that timing.

In the end, at a crossroads, we managed to catch up with the lead car. I took the radio one last time, trying to keep my cool.

"It's too risky. If we carry on like that, we could have an accident. Let us handle things."

That time, he listened to me. The driver of Ricardo's car slowed down, and we were able to get back into a normal formation for the last few kilometers.

At last, we arrived at the airport terminal. Ricardo got out of the car calmly, as if nothing had happened, and the CEO shook his head with an amused smile.

"Sorry about the chaos," Ricardo said, shaking my hand.

I couldn't help but smile, relieved that it was all over without a major incident. Ricardo and the CEO boarded their jet, while I leaned against the hood of my car, exhausted but satisfied. Another mission accomplished, and another story to tell.

Mission in Turkey: Between Two Continents

Arriving in Istanbul is like entering a city that lives between two worlds. Europe and Asia meet here, separated by the Bosphorus, a river shimmering with light and movement. But for us, the city represented above all a logistical challenge: two continents to secure, a local team to train, and a tight schedule.

As usual, I had arrived a week before the start of the mission to carry out some advance work. Istanbul is a chaotic, vibrant city, where every road seems to be hiding a surprise. My first task was to coordinate with local authorities and to form a team of Turkish drivers and security. Working with them was an enriching experience: Their professionalism and their local knowledge impressed me from the first days.

The hotel where we were staying was breathtaking. Situated on the Asian side of the Bosphorus, it dominated the river with a panoramic view over the water. Every morning, we crossed the river by boat to get to the European side, where most of the events took place. The journey was a moment of calm in our hectic days, a time to breathe in the salty air, while watching the comings and goings on the riverbanks.

Istanbul is not just a city; it's a patchwork of different periods, cultures, and influences, which all coexist harmoniously. Previously known as Byzantium, then Constantinople, before becoming Istanbul, it is the only metropolis in the world that spans two continents. Walking down the streets here was to go back through the centuries.

On the European side, you can admire the vestiges of the Byzantine Empire and Ottoman wonders like Saint-Sophie, whose huge domes tell a story of ingenuity and faith. Not far from there, the majestic Blue Mosque's minarets rise towards the sky, an ode to the power and beauty of the Ottoman past. Entering the mosque is to find yourself surrounded by sacred silence, fascinated by the many blue tiles decorating the walls, lit by the natural light that filters through the ornate windows.

But Istanbul is also about a modern buzz. At the heart of the souks, the perfume of spices fills the air: cinnamon, saffron, cumin... The stalls are overflowing with bright colors, from mountains of dried fruit and sugarcoated Turkish delights to shiny jewelry. The sellers called out with sincere smiles, always ready to negotiate.

And then there are the quays of the Bosphorus, where it feels like the city breathes. I loved making a stop there for a sandwich prepared in front of me from a street food stall. The sellers, armed with knives prepared generous portions of fried fresh fish, with crispy vegetables and lemon. The taste of these sandwiches, mixed with the noise of the waves and the cries of the seagulls, will always remain etched in my memory. These simple moments were a rare time of respite in a city that seems to be constantly on the go.

One of the key moments of this mission was an event organized by the company that Ricardo was the face of in a sumptuous place on the banks of the Bosphorus. This event brought together the cream of Istanbul, as well as eminent personalities from the world of Turkish politics, the arts, and cinema. Everything had been meticulously organized: We arrived by boat, drawing alongside a red carpet that led to a magnificent reception room. The sparkling lights, the elegant outfits, and the lively conversations gave the place an aura of rare sophistication.

Everyone was there for Ricardo. However, that evening, another event was secretly holding his attention: the final of the Champions' League, which was being played in Moscow between Manchester United and Chelsea.

Anticipating his interest, we had installed a screen backstage so that he could follow the match. At that time, there were no mobile phones that could show videos, and Ricardo couldn't imagine missing a match like that. So, true to himself, he discreetly slipped out of the dinner to go and watch the final.

I followed him, making sure I kept an eye on him while also watching the CEO, who was chatting to guests. Ricardo was absorbed by the match, analyzing each action as if he were still on the pitch. And suddenly, breaking the silence, he cried out, "Shit, he missed!"

This comment was about Nicolas Anelka, who had just missed his penalty shot at goal, sealing Chelsea's defeat against Manchester United. Ricardo, clearly frustrated, shook his head. "He must be gutted," he said, sharing both Anelka's pain and a touch of annoyance. That moment revealed his sincere attachment to football and his empathy for players, even after he retired.

Another high point of this mission was an organized visit to an isolated village in the center of Turkey. Ricardo and the CEO, with the team from the company, were due to play a football match with the children and to inaugurate a series of local activities. To cover security and to prepare for their arrival, I took a helicopter early in the morning to check things out.

At dawn, I boarded a yellow Bell 409, stationed on the helipad of the Kempinski hotel. As the city of Istanbul was waking up slowly, we flew over the Bosphorus, leaving the urban agitation behind us and heading out into the Turkish countryside. After around an hour's flight, we landed on some wasteland near the village.

The landing created instant an instant buzz. All the children of the village, maybe thirty or so, ran to see the helicopter. Some of them had left their games behind, others their morning tasks, all eyes riveted on the machine. They thought that Ricardo was on board. As I disembarked, their enthusiasm soon turned to disappointment. "It's not Ricardo," one said in a quiet voice, their faces gradually relaxing.

Not wanting to leave them frustrated, I followed them as they led me to a small outdoor café in the center of the village. There, under a tree, at a wooden table with four chairs, sat three elderly men, their faces tanned from years of working in the fields. They slowly sipped their Turkish coffee from small, delicate cups.

One of them signaled to the empty chair. I sat down without a word, and a young woman appeared, setting a cup of Turkish coffee in front of me. It was a tradition I couldn't refuse, although I had never drunk coffee before. I hesitated for a second before bringing the cup to my lips. The taste was intense, strong, but it was also a simple, clear moment. We remained sitting there, observing life slowly going on in the village, without exchanging more than a few glances.

An hour passed, and suddenly the air in the village changed. The noise of rotors filled the sky. The helicopter transporting Ricardo was approaching.

As Ricardo stepped down from it, the whole village seemed to light up. Children, delighted this time, rushed towards him, their bright smiles showing sincere joy. Local prominent citizens, wearing their traditional clothing, greeted him with respectful gestures. Ricardo, as usual, answered with warmth and simplicity, shaking hands and posing for photos.

The makeshift football pitch, surrounded by signs with the company logo, became the heart of the action. Ricardo played with the children, encouraging them, giving them advice, and sharing laughs with them. At one stage, one boy managed to score a goal, and Ricardo fell to the ground, pretending to be utterly dejected, to gales of laughter.

A few hours later, the time had come to leave. The helicopter set off again, and the excitement faded as quickly as it had risen. The children, who a few moments earlier had been running and laughing, were still looking up to the sky to follow the helicopter get further away. I watched their expressions, a mixture of joy and regret, and I wondered how many of them would remember this for the rest of their lives.

On board, the atmosphere was strangely calm. Ricardo, who was normally chatty after this kind of event, stared out the window, deep in thought. The rural countryside raced past below our feet: fields that went on forever, scattered houses, and in the distance, misty mountains.

The CEO was flipping through a file, probably a summary of the day and the expected media coverage. As for me, I was going through every step mentally, satisfied that all had gone without a glitch.

As we approached Istanbul, the city seemed to stretch out beneath the golden dusk sky. The setting sun was reflected on the Bosphorus, transforming the water into a bright orange and purple canvas. The bustle of the city came back to us slowly: horns, the buzz of the markets, and the indefinable energy that only Istanbul has.

We landed on the helipad of the Kempinski. As soon as the rotors stopped spinning, reality took over. The local security team was already in place to ensure a smooth transition, as Ricardo and the CEO headed to their rooms for a rest before the next engagement.

Later that evening, as the buzz of the day subsided, I bumped into Ricardo in one of the hotel bars. He was sitting alone, holding a glass of water, looking out a huge picture window that overlooked the Bosphorus.

I went over to him, hesitating about whether to interrupt his peace and quiet, but he turned to me with a smile.

"You know," he said quietly. "Those times with the children remind me where I come from. When I was a kid, if someone like me had come to play with us, it would have changed our world." He paused, his eyes locked on the water. "I just hope that they will keep that inside them, that they'll tell themselves that they can dream bigger."

I didn't answer right away, preferring to savor the sincerity of his words. That kind of interaction with Ricardo was rare but precious. Behind the worldwide icon was a man who was deeply attached to his values, aware of the impact he could have.

The last day of the mission was marked by a sumptuous reception on the roof of the Kempinski hotel, with a breathtaking view over the illuminated Bosphorus. Fairy lights hung on the terrasses, and the guests, dressed with understated elegance, sipped cocktails and spoke in low voices.

Ricardo, as usual, fluctuated between modesty and charisma. He greeted each guest with disarming simplicity, taking the time to thank them for being there. The CEO carried on strategic discussions, making sure that the event strengthened the image of his company in Turkey.

When Ricardo stepped onto the stage to say a few words, a respectful hush fell over the gathering.

"Football is universal," he began, his voice calm but firm. "It doesn't recognize borders, colors, or languages. It brings people together, like this evening. That's its real strength."

The applause that followed went on for a long time, mixing with the sound of the waves that gently lapped at the banks below us. It was a perfect end to a mission that had been intense but full of moments of humanity.

Early in the morning, Ricardo and the CEO took a private flight to return to Paris. The local team and I stayed for another few hours to finalize the last reports and tie up logistics.

As I left Istanbul, I thought back on the mission. It had been marked by a striking contrast between the chaotic beauty of the city, the simplicity of the remote villages, and the grandeur of the official events. But above and beyond the logistics and the protocols, it was the moments of humanity that held my attention: the children's eyes filled with wonder, Ricardo's passion for teaching them, and even the spontaneous shout backstage for Anelka's missed penalty.

Istanbul, with its colors, its smells, and its unique energy, had been much more than a backdrop. It was the reflection of what we had come to do: build bridges, between continents, between generations, and between dreams.

Ricardo's Biography: An Unexpected Trip to the Police Station

In La Défense, the company headquarters was buzzing that day as usual. But my mind was thrust into another reality when I received the call from Kaleb, one of my closest friends. His usually composed voice was shaking with unusual panic.

"They asked me questions about you," he said breathlessly. "A police inspector... They bugged you, and now they're listening in to me too because I'm flagged in the System for Reported Offenses."

The System for Reported Offenses, the well-known file where the police list individuals involved in affairs, even if they haven't been sentenced, had been a thorn in Kaleb's side for years. This call, filled with worry, only confirmed that something serious was going on.

"They want to know why you travel so much, you and Ricardo. They mentioned Israel, Canada, and even Sweden. What do you really do? Why these impromptu trips?"

Every word added another layer of worry. The idea of being listened to, having my life scrutinized by investigators, was unbearable to me. As soon as Kaleb hung up, I made a decision. No detours, no intermediaries. I left the head office and went straight to the 15th arrondissement police station, near the Gare Montparnasse.

When I arrived in front of it, I had no idea what kind of treatment I would receive. But one thing was sure: I wasn't planning on waiting for a summons to know what they had against me. If someone had accusations about me, I wanted to hear them face-to-face.

I asked to speak to Lieutenant Amir, the inspector in charge of the case. The agent on the desk gave me a confused look, visibly surprised that a "suspect" would present themselves.

"The lieutenant is not available," he answered me neutrally, in an almost detached way.

But I wasn't there to leave without doing what I came to do. Without waiting for his authorization, I went upstairs to the office where Amir's desk was. I had only just reached the hallway when I came across a man that I thought was him. He looked ordinary, but the calculating look in his eyes gave him away.

"Lieutenant Amir," I said, walking towards him. "You're investigating me. Let's go. Ask your questions now."

He stopped, visibly annoyed by my audacity.

"Sir, that's not how things work," he replied coldly. "When the time comes, you will be summoned."

His dry answer left no room for discussion. He turned and left, leaving me alone in the tight hallway. I went back down the stairs, frustrated but determined to find out what they had against me.

The following weeks were marked by underlying tension. Every unknown caller, every movement around me seemed to be charged with new suspicion. I carried on my trips for the company that Ricardo was the face of, as well as my personal missions, bearing in mind that any travel I made was probably being watched. Israel, Canada, Sweden... The investigators seemed to have gone through everything with a fine-tooth comb.

Then the summons arrived at last. I went to the police station, determined to face what they had to say to me. Lieutenant Amir's office was exactly as I had imagined: functional, impersonal, with computers lined up and folders stacked in a corner. He sat down at his desk, staring at me for a long time before beginning.

He started the interrogation with a series of apparently trivial questions. Where I had gone to in the last few months, with whom I had traveled, why my trips seemed so unpredictable. But very soon, his tone changed. He mentioned trips with Ricardo, my professional relationships, and even my security training.

"We know where you go. We know who you see. These unplanned trips, at the last minute... There's something to it," he said, staring at me.

I knew exactly what he was doing: He was trying to impress me, to unsettle me. But I had spent years learning to decode this kind of interrogation, detecting traps and keeping my cool under pressure. I let the insinuations go without defending myself, waiting until he finally got to the point.

After a long series of allusions and indirect questions, he finally gave up the information.

"This is about a flight. The manuscript of an unauthorized biography was stolen from the author's home. That manuscript was... let's say, controversial. And you, sir, are an ideal suspect."

According to Amir, my ties with Ricardo, my skills in "murky operations," and my past as a security operator made me an obvious suspect. Worse, he suspected that my employer may have orchestrated this theft to protect the image of his front man, ambassador for some of the company's brands.

"You work for a large group with unlimited resources," he insisted. "You have connections, training, and you are close to Ricardo. All that can't be a coincidence."

I couldn't help but smile. His accusations were absurd, and he knew it. But his aim wasn't to prove a thing. He wanted to push me into saying something, making a mistake.

"You have no proof," I retorted calmly. "And what you are saying has no basis. So, unless you have something specific, we're done here."

After a long pause, Amir finished the interview. He had nothing, and he knew it. The investigation never went anywhere, and the manuscript thief was never found. But this experience left an indelible mark on me.

Leaving the police station that day, I thought long and hard about what this affair meant. Being in the circle of a public figure like Ricardo had its advantages, but it also made me an easy target for unfounded suspicions. My past, my skills, and my relationships had been enough to place me at the heart of a groundless investigation.

As for what became of the manuscript, that remained a mystery. Perhaps it had been destroyed. Perhaps it was still lying somewhere, forgotten in the trunk of a car or a drawer. But when I thought about it, the conditions of this theft were so specific, so meticulously orchestrated, that it couldn't be the work of an amateur. The people who did this knew exactly what they were doing. They knew the times, the places, and above all, the priceless value of this document.

In any case, this story served as a lesson to me: In this line of work, the image that others have of you is sometimes as powerful as truth itself.

When I thought back to the investigation, I couldn't deny that, on paper, I was the perfect suspect. My background, my training, my ties to Ricardo, all that made me a target of suspicion for obvious reasons. I had spent years honing my skills: learning to disappear in a crowd, get around security systems, get into inaccessible places. These talents, which I owed to missions and intensive training, made me a formidable weapon. A weapon that few people around me really understood.

Add to that my proximity to Ricardo. We often went on trips, sometimes at the last minute, for reasons that may seem mysterious seen from the outside. And this relationship of proximity and trust, which I liked for its simplicity, also made me a choice target in an investigation like this.

As I went back up the road that day, a thought came to me. What if Lieutenant Amir wasn't totally wrong? He was right about one thing: I had the profile, I had the skills, I had the access. But what he didn't know was that I also had a code of conduct. And I have never broken that code. Not yet, at least.

I knew how much Ricardo wanted to protect his reputation, his legacy. So, yes, maybe if I had had a reason to get involved, if someone had asked me to get rid of that document, I could have done it. And I may even have done it without leaving a trace.

But the thing is, I have never told anyone the truth. Not Ricardo, not my friends, not people who, like Lieutenant Amir, wanted to read between the lines. Perhaps because they didn't need to know. Perhaps because some secrets are better kept in the shadows.

So, the manuscript has never resurfaced. And in this story, the culprit has never been found. Was it me? Was it somebody else? Part of me finds this ambiguity almost reassuring. After all, in my job, the truth is not always what it seems, and the best moves are those that leave everyone with doubts.

As I walked away from the police station, I couldn't help but smile. Not because the case was closed or because I had convinced Lieutenant Amir of my innocence. But because in this game of shadows and lights, I had done what I do best: left some doubt.

Who had stolen Ricardo's biography? I leave that question to history. Perhaps the answer matters less than the mystery itself. And maybe, just maybe, it's better that some things remain in the dark, where they can go on intriguing, fascinating and haunting those who are still trying to find answers.

V Private Life and Human Challenges

Invisible Sacrifices: The Price of an Extraordinary Life

Living in such a unique, fascinating world has a cost. A cost that few people can really imagine. This job, which has given me incredible opportunities, also cost me a part of myself. Every mission, every trip, and every victory leave an invisible weight behind. A weight that I carried silently.

Tiredness was my constant companion. Not only the kind of tiredness that goes away with a good night's sleep. No, it was deep exhaustion, rooted in years of adrenaline, sleepless nights, and tension. Hours of sleep were rare, broken, and often interrupted by abrupt awakenings, my mind always on high alert. Even the most luxurious hotels couldn't give me real rest. Their comfort just masked the reality: I never really slept.

But physical fatigue is only part of the problem. The isolation was harder to deal with. For years, my life didn't belong to my loved ones but to my work. The missed calls, the messages I never replied to, the forgotten birthdays... I lived in a bubble, disconnected from normal relationships. Sometimes, I wondered what my family really thought of me. Did they understand why I was never there? Or had they just learnt to live without me?

The hardest thing was realizing that I had become a stranger to them. I remember a rare moment in Paris, when at last I had a few days for myself. I tried to make up for lost time with an old friend. But our conversations, which used to be smooth and spontaneous, had become awkward. My world was too far from theirs. That gap, that uncomfortable silence between us, struck me more than ever before. That was the price to pay.

To a lot of people, my life seemed enviable. Private jets to cross continents, suites in the most luxurious hotels in the world, meals in Michelin-starred restaurants... From the outside, all this seemed like a dream life. But in truth, that luxury was just a front. A façade behind which was hidden a very different reality.

The private jets weren't spaces for relaxing in but rather flying offices. Every flight was an extension of work. We spent hours going over files, revising plans, coordinating teams. No champagne, no relaxation. Just constant tension, more figures to go through, or maps, or critical information.

As for five-star hotels, they were anything but a sanctuary. Behind the silent hallways and spotless sheets, I saw potential threats. An open window, an unmonitored hallway... each detail could become a problem. Even in the most secure places, I could never let down my guard. That constant vigilance stole more nights' sleep from me than I care to admit.

And then, there were the missions themselves. Where appearances of luxury met the realities on the ground. One minute, we were discussing strategy in an air-conditioned office. The next we were crossing an area where the very idea of security seemed absent. That contrast, between artificial comfort and the harsh reality of the missions, sometimes became almost absurd. But that was the whole duality of my job: one foot in luxury, the other in chaos.

Moving from one continent to another, one country to another was routine for me. I could take off from Paris one morning, be in the middle of an Asian city in the evening, and a few days later, walking in a remote village where time seemed to have stopped. That pace, which was both exciting and unsettling, required a constant ability to adapt: to cultures, customs, religions, which were sometimes radically different.

My upbringing helped me to navigate through these many worlds. With a Muslim father and a Catholic mother, I grew up in an environment where diversity was not only tolerated but valued. That double culture taught me to respect the beliefs and the traditions of others, to listen before judging, and to observe before acting.

But this life of constant trips also made me face striking differences. One of the most memorable examples was the issue of access to water. During a mission in Africa, I visited a village where every drop of water was precious. Women walked for hours under the burning sun to fill jerry cans with water from a community well. Running water, for them, was nothing but a dream. That very evening, I went back to a hotel where an Olympic swimming pool was filled with crystal clear water.

Another source of reflection was the clash between France and China. I often found myself in the middle of this economic water, where a French multinational, armed with its values and its know-how, took on a complex and formidably effective Chinese system. It wasn't just a matter of commercial competition. It was a cultural clash, a confrontation between two visions of the world.

France, where I grew up, represented for me the culture of refinement, reflection, and debate. A country where innovation went hand in hand with a certain slow pace, almost poetic in approach. China, on the other hand, was fast, implacable, and deeply pragmatic. Over there, I learnt what adaptation, hard work, and collective discipline meant. That country, where I became a man, forged my character in a way I could never have imagined.

These two cultures, both totally magnificent and in total opposition, shaped my perception of the world. In the context of the economic war between the Altéone Group and Wang Industries, they clashed relentlessly. France, with its structure and its rules, was trying to navigate in an environment where China played with its own codes, which were often informal and hard to anticipate.

But that cultural clash also taught me something essential: These differences, far from being obstacles, can be a source of enrichment. I witnessed times when the mutual respect between the French and Chinese teams allowed us to find unexpected solutions. Those experiences reminded me that, in spite of divergences, there is always common ground, if you take the time to look for it.

I also remember an encounter in Cuba. It was with a young woman, who was an accountant in a small company. She earned the equivalent of 50 euros per month. For me, coming from a world where expenses could reach thousands of euros in just a few days, that figure was unthinkable. I asked her how she managed to survive on so little.

She answered me with an honest smile, "My life is simple. I go to work, I go home, I look after my mother, and then I go out dancing. Every day is the same thing, but I don't need anything else."

Her words stuck with me. She went on, "The more things you have, the more problems you have. Every possession, every object adds to the stress. I have almost nothing, so I have almost no worries."

That perspective, although very far from mine, was filled with profound truth. In the countries where I had worked, I had often observed that those who had the least also seemed to be those who lived the lightest. That young women reminded me that wealth is not a matter of possessions but of freedom with regard to our possessions.

Through all these experiences, I realized that my life was going to be a constant balancing exercise. Between vigilance and exhaustion, between luxury and sacrifices, between professional demands and moral issues. Every day, I juggled with these opposing forces, trying to maintain a fragile stability.

In spite of everything, I knew why I was doing this job. It wasn't for the luxury, not for the adrenaline. It was for the moments when everything aligned. Successful missions, lives that were protected, dreams achieved... Those moments, which were rare yet precious, were worth all the sacrifices. And even if that life took a lot out of me, it also gave me lessons that I will never forget.

I don't regret anything, because these experiences, as challenging as they were, allowed me to see the world from a unique angle. They gave me a passport to deeper understanding of human dynamics, cultures, and the tensions that shape our fear. That constant mix of adaptability, introspection, and perseverance has enriched my life more than I could ever have imagined.

Looking back, I realize that every sacrifice had meaning. The sleepless nights, the dangers, the moments of isolation... all this was part of a bigger picture. A picture where I had a mission to accomplish: protecting, supporting, and sometimes representing those who were relying on me to move their projects or their ideals forward.

This life also taught me to look at the world with open eyes. The disparities I observed – between wealth and poverty, luxury and need, freedom and oppression – left an indelible mark on me. But they also taught me the importance of grit and of hope.

When I think back to the Cuban woman, with her paltry salary and her sincere smile, I understand that happiness is not a matter of material circumstances but rather of attitude. She showed me that it is possible to dance in spite of everything, to be at peace with what we have, and to find meaning in little things.

That lesson echoes in my own life. In a world of extreme contrasts, where I went from a private jet to a village without electricity, I was able to appreciate every moment for what it was. The simple moments, like sharing a drink with a stranger in a remote place, often had more value than the most luxurious receptions.

But when I think back on all this, one question keeps coming back: What did I learn from that life?

What did I accomplish? And more importantly, how can I use these experiences to keep on moving forward?

The world remains a place of contradictions, tensions, and challenges. But it is also a place of infinite possibilities. If this life has taught me anything, it's that differences, far from being barriers, are bridges. Whether it is between cultures, between generations, or between rich and poor, there is always room to understand each other and to come together.

I keep on walking that line, between cultures, between challenges, between the lessons of the past and hopes for the future. And I don't regret anything. On the contrary, I am grateful.

But that was just the start of my adventures. This unique path led me to even more unlikely horizons. It led me to the high-tech offices of Silicon Valley, where I saw the future designed at dizzying speed. In the Tesla factories, where mechanics and vision seem to fuse in perfect choreography.

It led me to the vast open spaces of Australia, where the challenges of the mining industry and hostile environments require constant adaptation. Pharmaceutical laboratories of the biggest global companies, where the fight against invisible illnesses plays out every day.

And also, to places where humanitarian urgency dominates everything: the basements of Bakhmut in Ukraine turned into field hospitals during the Russian invasion, where every instant counted to save lives. The beaches of Gaza, where tensions and hope coexist in a fragile balance. Or even, during Hurricane Kenneth, the flooded fields infested with Islamist terrorists in Macomia in Mozambique, where man and nature seem to be working together to defy any possibility of survival.

It also took me to the dark alleys of Mexico City, where shadows in the night hide brutal violence, exacerbated by the horror of kidnappings for ransom. There, I witnessed humanity torn apart by constant fear, lives changed in an instant, and the extreme violence, which has become a business that is both cold and lucrative. These places reminded me that, behind every scene of chaos, there are souls that survive, resist, and hope.

These adventures followed one another, and each of them added a new page to the story of my life, constantly reminding me that in the darkest places, there is always a light you can find – and often, a light that you can bring.

LIAM MONCLAIR LLC

email: contact@liammonclair.com